I unlatched the shed and went inside. Garry followed me in and stood in the doorway. He was muttering on about the poster and the project when I silenced him with a shocked gasp. Cherokee's box was not on the workbench. It had somehow tumbled off to one side and was lying wedged between the corner of the bench and the panelled wall of the shed itself. The flaps of the box were pointing downwards. I knew without looking she wasn't inside.

'Shut the door!' I shouted. 'And be careful where you're standing!'

'What?' he said.

'Gazza, shut the door!'

I pointed to the box. Gazza recognized the danger and did as instructed.

Slowly I crouched down into the shadows. 'She's on the floor somewhere. She might be hurt. You check behind the mower; I'll look behind the workbench.'

For several minutes we searched in vain, crawling about on our hands and knees and poking our fingers into all the little places a pigeon might squeeze its hollow-boned body. We found nothing. Not a single feather . . .

D0877250

CHRIS d'LACEY

FLY, CHEROKEE, FLY

CORGI BOOKS

FLY, CHEROKEE, FLY
A CORGI BOOK : 0 552 547891

First published as a Corgi Yearling 1998

PRINTING HISTORY
Corgi edition published 2002

1 3 5 7 9 10 8 6 4 2

Set in 12/15.5pt Palatino by
Phoenix Typesetting, Ilkley, West Yorkshire

Corgi Books are published by Transworld Publishers,
61–63 Uxbridge Road, London W5 5SA,
a division of The Random House Group Ltd,
in Australia by Random House Australia (Pty) Ltd,
20 Alfred Street, Milsons Point, Sydney, NSW 2061, Australia,
in New Zealand by Random House New Zealand Ltd,
18 Poland Road, Glenfield, Auckland 10, New Zealand
and in South Africa by Random House (Pty) Ltd,
Endulini, 5a Jubilee Road, Parktown 2193, South Africa

Printed and bound in Great Britain by
Cox & Wyman Ltd, Reading, Berkshire

*for Greg & Gigi and all they raised,
and Megan, who hatched the egg*

CHAPTER ONE

I found Cherokee Wonder on Great Elms Park. It was the day before Mum's birthday, which means it's about six months, two weeks and three days ago now. Ages, I suppose. But loads of people still ask me about her. We ought to have a sign up outside our house saying: 'Darryl Otterwell, youngest pigeon fancier in Aylestone lives here'. I bet if we did, people would be knocking on the door all day. And then Mum would have to make endless cups of tea and I'd have to tell the story *all over again*. Mr Tompkins, my teacher, said I should write the story down because that way I wouldn't get fed up telling it. I must have told it a million times already, but a million and one won't hurt, I suppose.

It started like this: me and Garry Taylor were playing football in the park. I was in goal. I'm always in goal. Garry thinks he's going to be a striker for England. He likes to prove it by blasting in his 'break the net' shots, which means I have to run miles to fetch the ball. On the night I found Cherokee, the ball had rolled up right to the hedgerows near the bowling greens. And there she was, my special pigeon, hiding in the leaf mould under a hedge.

'What you looking at, Dazza?' Garry shouted, practising his goal-scoring celebration wiggle.

I waved him to be quiet, which brought him pounding up beside me, of course. I pointed to the huddled shape among the leaves. He went white with fear and grabbed the ball off me. 'Is it a rat?' he hissed, backing off.

'A rat with feathers?' I tutted at him.

Garry let out a defensive sniff. He turned his collar up just in case.

I crouched down slowly. Cherokee was sitting like a nesting bird, but I couldn't see any sign of eggs. She didn't look well. Her breast was puffed out as if she was cold and her feathers looked dull and broken in places. I pushed my hands forward to pick her up. She made a wooing noise and cocked her head. Her copper eye blinked and she tried to stand. 'I won't hurt you,' I whispered, and closed my hands around her. She stretched a pink foot out, but she didn't struggle.

'If you get bitten and die,' said Garry, 'can I have those trainers with the ticks on the ankles?'

'Quiet,' I shushed him, easing Cherokee out into the open. She blinked again as the light fell on her.

'I've got a joke,' said Garry, raising his hand like I was Mr Tompkins, our English teacher at school. 'What's black and white and green all over?'

'Ha, ha,' I replied. I knew he meant the pigeon. She wasn't like the normal grey ones you see. Her wings were a shiny blue-black colour. But her head and breast and tail were white. What you could see of them was white, anyway. Her undersides were covered in a gooey green slime. It was trickling through my fingers like an ice-cream topping. I found out later it was pigeon diarrhoea.

'What you gonna do with it, then?' asked

Garry. He was juggling the football and didn't look up.

I ran my thumb down the side of her neck. Her feathers felt soft and warm and waxy. I'd never really held a bird before. She weighed about as much as a tennis ball. There was only one thing I could do, really.

'Fly!' I breathed, and threw her up into the pale-blue sky. I knew it was wrong as soon as I'd done it. Cherokee hadn't got the strength to fly. She flapped like mad and nose-dived to earth. Groggily, she picked herself up off the ground, limped across a short stretch of grass to a rose-bed, fell off the verge and settled in the dirt in a miserable huddle.

'Rubbish,' sniffed Gazza.

But I didn't really hear him. I was back at Cherokee's side again. When I picked her up this time I didn't let her go. 'I'm taking you home,' I told her quietly. She shivered and squashed her head into her breast.

'He's gonna put you on a stick and roast you,' said Garry.

I gave him a glare that could wipe the smirk off a waxworks dummy and started down the path towards Great Elms Road.

'Well you can't look after it, can you?' he said,

bouncing the ball on the path behind me. 'Who wants a useless pigeon, anyway?'

'Mum'll know what to do,' I sniffed.

Garry made a sort of humming noise.

I brought Cherokee up dead close to my face. 'My mum'll know what to do,' I whispered.

CHAPTER TWO

'OUT!'

'But Mu-um?'

'No buts. Out. And don't you "Mum" me, Darryl Otterwell. Get that filthy thing out of my kitchen before it does something nasty on my worktop. Look at it, it's covered. And look at your sweater! How, pray, am I supposed to clean that? You put that bird back EXACTLY where you found it, then get undressed and straight into the bath!'

'You mean he has to get undressed in the

park?' asked Garry. I rolled my eyes skywards and gave him a kick.

Mum gave Garry a frosty glare. 'Haven't you got a home to go to, Garry Taylor?'

'Darryl said I could stay for tea.'

'Darryl isn't having any TEA!' Mum bellowed.

'I wonder what pigeons have for *their* tea,' said a voice. It was my little sister, Natalie. She was sitting at the table with her colouring books. 'I *wonder* if they like baked beans,' she mused.

Mum heaved a sigh and shook her head. For a moment, I thought she was going to soften. Then Garry sniffed and she turned on us again. 'Well? What are you pair waiting for – Christmas?'

'But it can't fly, Mum.'

'It crashes,' Garry added.

'It's a wild bird,' Mum said sternly. 'Wild things belong out there, in the wild.' She uncrossed her arms and pointed to the door. As if by magic, it rattled open.

'Evening all!' Dad's voice came booming down the hall.

Natalie ran to meet him. 'Daddy! Daddy! Darryl's got a pigeon!'

'Ooh, I hope it's a fat one,' said Dad. 'I just fancy some pigeon pie for tea.'

'Yurrgghh,' went Garry, aiming a finger down his throat.

'Where is it, then?' said Dad, holding Natalie by the wrists and swinging her to and fro down the hall.

'It's here, Dad,' I blurted, before Mum could cut in. 'I only want to help it. I don't want to keep it. It's hurt. I think it's broken its wing.' I held Cherokee up for Dad to see.

'Pretty,' he said. 'Where'd you find it? The park?'

'Don't encourage him,' Mum said quietly. But I was winning the battle. I told Dad everything.

'Hmm,' he hummed. 'Well, strictly speaking your mum's right, Darryl. You really ought to put it back in the park. Pigeons are officially classed as vermin. Not many people like them, you know.'

'That bag lady from number nineteen does,' said Garry. 'She's always feeding the birds in town.'

'I *wonder* what a bag lady keeps in her bag,' said Natalie.

'Natalie, go and wash your hands,' said Mum. 'Darryl, you heard what your father said.

Take the bird away and don't be long about it.'

My shoulders dropped. Dad tousled my hair. 'It's for the best,' he said, and stroked the bird's back. The contact made Cherokee shuffle a little. She thrust a clawed foot between my fingers.

'Hang on,' said Dad. 'What's that by her foot?' he pointed to something on Cherokee's leg: a blue plastic ring. It was the first time I'd noticed it.

'What's that for?' I asked, wiping dirt off the ring. Underneath the dirt was some tiny writing.

Dad frowned in thought. 'Well, this changes everything.'

'Pardon?' said Mum.

'It's got a ring on,' said Dad.

'Is it married?' Garry asked.

Dad laughed and shook his head. 'Not married, Garry, but it's certainly kept. This is a racing pigeon you've found. It could be valuable. We ought to try and find out who it belongs to.'

'Yes!' I exclaimed. I looked at Mum.

'It's a conspiracy,' she sighed. 'I don't know why I bother.'

'Put the bird in the shed for now,' said Dad. 'After tea, I'll tell you where to take it.'

CHAPTER THREE

'This is it,' said Garry. 'Forty-seven St Wilfred's Road. There it is, look! There's the yellow star!'

I'd already seen it – and the drive that looked like a patchwork quilt, all red and blue and yellow pavers. It was just the way that Dad had described it: an old stone cottage with a star on the roof.

'Why?' we'd asked. 'What's the star for?'

But Dad had just smiled the way he does, scribbled a name on a scrap of paper and pushed it across the table towards us.

'Alf Duckins?' I'd said.

Dad gave me a wink. 'He'll know what to do with your bird.'

'P'r'aps he's a pilot,' Garry suggested, as we stood at the gate to Alf Duckins' drive. 'They put stars on their planes, don't they?'

'Umm,' I grunted, but I wasn't really listening. I was gazing up at the dusky sky. Ten or twelve large birds were gliding around. They fluttered in to land on the roof of the garage, then took off and disappeared over the back.

'Pigeons!' shouted Garry, like a sailor spotting land.

I touched the shoe-box under my arm. 'Come on,' I said, unlatching the gate, 'and don't do anything stupid, Gazza.'

'As if,' he said with an indignant sniff, playing hopscotch all the way up the drive. He reached the door first. I made him knock.

'It's creepy is this,' he said, not meaning it. 'What if he's really old and grumpy? What if he's a filthy, smelly tramp? What if—'

Suddenly we knew. The door burst open and a man wearing baggy grey tracksuit bottoms and a holey jumper appeared on the step. He was as old and shaggy as my grandad's dog and he smelled a bit like rotting straw. Garry stepped back and held his nose. 'What do you pair want?' the old man snapped. 'I saw you jigging around on my drive. Go on, shove it. Or I'll get the law.'

'Are you Mr Duckins?' I asked with a gulp.

'Who wants to know?'

'We do,' said Garry, 'or we wouldn't be asking.'

The old man gave us a beady stare. He pushed up his sleeves and looked as if he might clip Garry round the ear. I glanced at his jumper. There were feathers sticking to it. 'Please, Mr Duckins. We've brought you a bird.'

'I've got plenty,' he said. 'Now hoppit – or else.' He pointed a leathery finger down the path.

'It's got a ring on,' I blurted. 'My dad says it's a racer.'

'It's worth TONS of money,' Garry chipped in.

Alf Duckins twitched. His eyes fell on the shoe-box.

I bit my lip and opened the box. Cherokee looked up. She was shaking slightly. Alf Duckins muttered something mean about 'kids', then lifted her gently out of the box. He held her tightly in one rough hand, locking his fingers around her back so she couldn't spread her wings and try to fly off.

18

'Hmm,' he mumbled, lifting her beak. 'Not a bad looking hen is that.'

'Hen?' hissed Garry. 'It's not a *hen*.'

'How would you know?' Alf Duckins sneered.

Garry lifted his shoulders. 'It doesn't go cluck.'

'Not a farm hen, you Charlie!' The blast was so loud it nearly knocked Garry over.

'You mean it's a female?' I said, surprised. Up until then, I'd thought Cherokee was a male.

'Aye,' said Mr Duckins, 'like I said, a hen. Cocks have a larger, rougher wattle.'

'A what-ul?' asked Garry.

'The white bit at the top of her beak,' Alf grunted.

Before I had the chance to examine her wattle, Mr Duckins took hold of Cherokee's wing and stretched it, fan-like, as far as it would go. 'I s'pose you know this wing's no good?' He felt her shoulder. 'Bust and reset. Awkward by the look of it. She's not in any pain. Exhausted, more like.' He turned her over and a look of surprise spread across his wrinkles. 'Hello,' he said, 'it's one of Spigott's.'

I looked at Garry. He looked back and shrugged.

Mr Duckins showed us the underside of the wing. Some sort of code had been stamped on the feathers. 'That's Spigott's, that is. No doubt about it. He's the biggest flying man for miles around. Lives in Barrowmoor, just up the road. You're right, this hen could be worth a few quid. I s'pose you'll be wanting me to ring Spigott for you?'

'Yes, please,' I said. I was almost breathless. Cherokee was saved. She was going home.

'Do we get a reward?' Garry piped up.

'From Lenny Spigott?' Mr Duckins snorted. 'He might be good with birds, but he doesn't like kids.'

'We just want to help her,' I said importantly.

Mr Duckins gave me a careful look. 'Aye, well,' he mumbled, 'we'll see about that.' He laid Cherokee gently back into the box. 'Come on, then. Be sharp. You'd better come through.'

'You mean—?'

'Aye, get a move on. The light's fading and my birds want a feed.'

'Ace!' said Garry. 'Have you got some bread?'

Alf Duckins grimaced. I could tell he was thinking it might be a mistake letting a boy like Garry Taylor near his pigeons. But I got the feeling he liked me a bit. As we walked through the house towards a sliding glass door that led out into the garden he said, 'In a corner of the loft you'll find a bin of grain. You can feed them some of that. But not too much. I don't want them looking like Christmas puddings. They've a big race, Saturday. Cross Channel, from France.'

'Brilliant,' said Garry, already through the door and out on to the patio.

'Oi!'

Garry winced and turned around. Mr Duckins jabbed a finger in my direction. 'I said *he* could feed them.'

Garry shoved his hands in the pockets of his jeans. 'What can I do, then?'

'Keep a look-out for Carrots.'

'What?' said Garry. He stared at me.

I didn't know what Mr Duckins meant either. But there wasn't any time to ask. The sun was dipping behind the trees. I pushed past Garry and headed for the pigeon loft at the top end of the garden.

Behind us, Alf Duckins picked up the phone.

CHAPTER FOUR

'He's got a bag on with me,' Garry grumbled to himself as we strolled across the patio and climbed three crumbling steps to the lawn. He flicked a blade of grass off the end of his thumb. 'Who wants to feed his stupid pigeons anyway? Pigeons are rubbish. Just like OLD people. Except they're worse. They're *double* rubbish.'

'Shut up,' I hissed. 'What if he hears you?' I cast a worried look back over my shoulder. Mr Duckins was sitting in a cane armchair, just inside the patio door. He was nodding, but not saying much into the phone.

'How can he hear me?' Garry scoffed. 'Everybody knows old people are deaf.' To prove it, he loosed off three wolf yells. A few pigeons that were pecking at the edge of the lawn took off with a frightened clattering of wings. They wheeled through the sky towards the roof of the house and settled with a scrimmage of claws on the slates. As they landed, another lot fluttered to the chimney-stack. Everywhere, pigeons cooed their annoyance. I couldn't blame them. I knew how they felt. But I could do more than coo at Garry Taylor.

'Pack it in,' I growled, and aimed a punch at his shoulder. He saw me coming and swerved away fast.

'How many do you think he's got?' he said, skipping backwards, eyes on the roof.

'How should I know? Hundreds. What does it matter?'

I could sense Garry's mind beginning to tick. 'If you get pecked to death when you're feeding them, can I have your T-shirt with SPLAT! written on it?'

'No,' I said firmly and slowed to a halt as . . . SPLAT! Garry backed into the wall of the loft. A few noisy protests rose from inside. Two birds whooshed through the open door.

'Thanks for the warning,' Garry moaned, rubbing a hand against the back of his head. He turned and examined what he'd hit. 'Wow, do you think he supports Newcastle United or something?'

'As if,' I scoffed. But I could see what he meant. The pigeon loft was painted in black and white stripes, the same as Newcastle United's strip. I made a note to ask Mr Duckins about it. He didn't look the type who followed football to me.

I'd never been this close to a pigeon loft before. It was a bit like investigating an alien spaceship: I wasn't *quite* sure what waited through the door. From the outside, the loft was like a great long potting shed. It was raised off the ground on pillars of bricks with a little flight of steps leading up to the door. On either side of the door was a sort of window – except there wasn't any glass, just lots of wooden slats. Near the windows, quite high, was a set of arched holes, each with a little landing board. I reached up and poked my hand through a hole. Dangling behind it was a row of wires.

'It's a prison,' said Garry, spotting the wires too.

'Don't be stupid,' I said, but he was almost right. While we stood there, arguing, a big brown bird with white tail-feathers landed on a board just by my hand. It dipped its head and waddled through the hole. The wires jangled. The sound of flight echoed deep within the loft, followed by a rasping, cooing sound. I reached up and felt the wires again.

'It's a trap,' I said. 'You can push the wires inwards but you can't pull them out.'

'What's the use of that?' Garry said, confused.

'Dunno,' I shrugged. Something else to ask Mr Duckins. That reminded me – feeding. I climbed the steps to the open door.

'What's it like?' asked Garry.

I shrugged. 'Not much. Two compartments with perches and stuff.'

'Smart. Let's have a see.'

Before I could stop him he was bounding up the steps and trying to push past me. 'Back off,' I said, and shoved him down again. I can wrestle Garry to the ground with ease. It felt a bit cruel, keeping him out like that, but I knew if I let him into the loft he would only stick his foot through the floor or something.

'Come on, Dazza. I found the bird as well.'

'No, you didn't. And you heard what Mr

Duckins said. You're supposed to be looking for carrots.'

Garry screwed up his face and peered round the garden. A few odd birds were back on the lawn. 'That's mental, that is. No-one guards against *carrots*.'

'Well, just keep a look out for . . . anything,' I said. 'I'm going to get the food. I'll be out in a minute.' I stood to attention and gave him a salute.

'Huh,' he muttered, and turned to stand guard.

Despite the unglazed windows it was warm inside the loft, a bit like being in my gran's summer-house. There was a funny sort of sawdusty smell about the place, mixed with a slight whiff of disinfectant. Glancing at the floor I could understand why. It was covered with grit and garden bits and millions of dried-up pigeon droppings. It scrunched underfoot as I moved about.

I walked down to the biggest compartment first. There were loads of v-shaped perches on the wall and a set of box perches like the pigeon-holes outside the staff room at school. *Pigeon-holes*. I grinned and nodded to myself. Now I knew why they called them that. There was a little rack of shelves at that end, too. They were loaded up with scrapers and cage fronts and stuff, and what looked like medicines on the highest shelf. I'd never imagined that pigeons could get sick. I wondered what you gave one for a broken wing.

Turning round, I saw the food bin was at the opposite end of the loft – in a corner, like Mr Duckins had said. To get there, I had to walk down a corridor stacked high on one side with wooden cages. They looked like a wall of rabbit hutches. Each of the cages had two dowelled doors – one was open, one was shut, staggered at each of the separate levels. I was halfway down the corridor when a bird appeared in the top middle box. It was the one I'd seen flying in through the trap. I stopped walking. The brown bird cocked its head a few times. There was a nervous glint in its round copper eye. 'It's all right,' I whispered, 'I'm not going to hurt you.' I took a half-step forward. The bird made a noise and shuffled sideways, its pink feet clinging to the bottom of the door. I walked on until I drew level with it. Then I took a chance and looked at it squarely. I could see it wasn't as young as Cherokee. Its big white nose was old and crusty and the feathers round its beak had seen better times. It stretched its neck and looked at me again. 'You're beautiful,' I told it, and lifted a finger, hoping it would let me stroke its breast. 'Woo,' it went, in throaty complaint, then turned and hopped into the back of its cage.

I hurried to the corn-bin and lifted the lid. Inside was a colourful mixture of grains: maize, peas, beans and seeds. I dug my hand in deep and let them tumble through my fingers. Behind me, I heard a scrabbling sound. The old bird was back at the cage front again. 'Tea-time,' I told him with a grin on my face. And scooping up some food in a boiled-sweet tin, I walked down the corridor, rattling it at him.

The old bird followed me out of the loft. I dropped a few grains and he started to peck.

'Watch out!' said Garry, from the far side of the lawn. He pointed at the sky. I looked up and felt my knees go wobbly. A huge flock of birds was descending fast. 'Chuck the food!' Garry flapped. I didn't need prompting. I sprayed the whole tin in a sweeping arc and ran across the lawn to join Garry by a flower-bed. The birds rained down like great grey hailstones. Forty or fifty at least. Just like the middle of Trafalgar Square.

'Wow, look at them go,' said Garry.

I nodded. They certainly could eat fast. Their beaks were going like little road-diggers. It took them less than thirty seconds to completely clear the lawn.

'I don't think you've given them enough,' said Garry as the nearest of the birds began to potter towards us. I turned the tin upside down and shook it. The birds dashed forward like an incoming tide.

Garry leaned over and snatched the tin. 'I'll get some more,' he said, and was gone.

'Gazza, wait!' I cried, but I couldn't move to stop him. Mr Duckins wouldn't thank me if I squashed a prize pigeon. Besides, what harm could Garry do?

As it happened, for once, no harm at all. He'd been inside the pigeon loft about three seconds when he let out an awful hollering noise. The birds lifted from the lawn in a frantic heap. I looked towards the loft. Garry was pounding down the steps, preceded by a very large ginger cat. The cat had a feather flagging off its tail. It bolted down the garden and nearly ran straight into Mr Duckins.

'Git out!' he roared, and harried it back towards Garry once more. Garry went after it, flailing his arms. The startled cat found a gap in the fence and wiggled through almost flat to the ground. The loose feather spiralled up into the sky. Calm returned to the garden again.

'Carrots!' said Garry, pointing after the cat. His face was a picture of boyish triumph.

'Aye, well done,' Mr Duckins panted, wiping a sleeve across his forehead. He felt for the arm of the garden bench and lowered himself with a heavy thump. He was wheezing badly and his face was red.

'Shall I get you a drink of water, Mr Duckins?'

The old man shook his head a few times. He patted his chest and made a snorting sound. 'Now then, about this bird.'

'Yes,' I said eagerly.

'Spigott doesn't want it.'

I looked open-mouthed at Garry. 'Why?' Garry asked.

Mr Duckins reached down and picked a feather off the ground. 'Crocked bird's no good to anyone, lad. Not even to itself. Chances are she's never going to fly again. Even if she does, she can't win races. That's the way it is with pigeons. Pity, really. Spigott says she was a good hen, once.'

'Won't you look after her, then, Mr Duckins?'

Alf Duckins gave me a pained look. 'You

can leave her with me. I'll do what's right.'

I shuffled my feet and looked awkwardly at Garry. 'Are you going to wring its neck?' Garry blurted out loud.

I turned and was set to blast him for a moment. But I couldn't bring myself to say anything at all. That thought had been in my mind as well. Only I hadn't had the courage to voice it. Surely Mr Duckins wasn't going to kill her?

'It's an invalid,' he said. 'You've done what you can.'

'You can't kill her,' I stammered, finding my voice. 'Please, Mr Duckins. You can't do that. What if it was one of your best birds? What if it was that brown one with the white tail-feathers?'

I pointed a finger at the pigeon loft. Alf gave me a thoughtful, searching look. There was something going on behind his pale grey eyes. Something he wasn't going to share with me then. 'Flying men don't keep pets,' he said.

'We do,' said Garry, with a spark of defiance.

'That's right,' I agreed, backing him up. 'If Mr Spigott doesn't want her, we'll keep her ourselves.'

'But she's *crocked*,' Alf said, throwing his hands up in despair.

Garry folded his arms. I did the same.

Mr Duckins sighed and shook his head. He stood up and dusted his pants with his hand. 'It's not like keeping a budgie, you know. You can't put her in a cage and teach her to talk.'

We both just shrugged. Alf sighed again.

'All right, go and fetch her. She's just on the patio. We'd better get her cleaned up before night falls.'

'I'll go,' said Garry, and galloped off towards the house.

Mr Duckins muttered something underneath his breath. He took off his cap and stared at the gallery of birds on the roof.

'Thanks,' I said shyly, picking my fingers. 'I really like her, Mr Duckins. I'll look after her. I promise.'

Alf grunted and touched a finger to his nose. 'I must be barmy. Dunno what Spigott would say if he knew. Strictly by the book, you're nabbing his bird. But if he wants her put down, I can't see the harm in it. Keep it to yourself all the same though, lad.'

I nodded. Garry came pounding up beside us.

He raised the lid on Cherokee's shoe-box. 'She's a mess,' Alf sighed. 'In more ways than one.' He lifted her out and preened her feathers. 'Here y'are,' he said to me, handing her over, making sure I held her correctly. 'Let her get used to you. She belongs to you now. She'll always stay tame if you handle her proper. Right, follow me. First stop, bath.'

With that Mr Duckins led us back to the loft. He got an old brown bucket and filled it with water from an outside tap, then sprinkled something called *Feather Bloom* in it. He took Cherokee from me and dipped her in the bucket, ruffling her feathers to bring out the dirt. The water turned green in a matter of seconds. We had to change it twice before she really came clean.

She looked like a waterlogged sock when we'd finished. 'Too cold to let her dry out naturally,' said Alf, noting the lengthening shadows in the garden. He turned and plodded back into the loft. When he emerged a few moments later, he had a towel over one hand and another tin of pigeon food tight in the other. He thrust the food in Garry's direction. 'Nice and steady, so they all get something.' Garry's face lit up. He was really chuffed. Some reward, I suppose, for rousting

Carrots. As Garry walked away sowing seed across the garden, Mr Duckins sniffed and lifted the towel. Underneath the towel was an old hairdrier.

'She's had this before,' he said with a grin, playing the warm air across Cherokee's feathers. I tilted her slightly and she lifted a wing, letting Alf get to the damper feathers on the side of her body. For the first time I saw the bump at her shoulder – the break that had almost condemned her to death. I shuddered and tried not to think about it. She was safe now, that was all that mattered. Safe from the hands of Lenny Spigott.

But the battle wasn't quite over yet. When I got home, I still had to persuade Mum and Dad to let me keep Cherokee. I knew exactly what Mum was going to say, 'Darryl, you don't know the first *thing* about keeping pigeons!' So while Cherokee was coming back to dryness, I asked Alf as many questions as I could.

There was one thing I almost forgot to ask. I remembered it while we were saying good-bye. 'Mr Duckins?' I said. 'Can I ask you a question?'

'Another one?' said Alf. 'My brain's about to burst!'

'When you were talking to Lenny Spigott, did he tell you the pigeon's name?'

'Name?' said Alf, looking at me strangely. He tapped the side of his foot against the porch. 'Nobody gives their pigeons *names*.'

CHAPTER FIVE

'Darryl, you don't know the first *thing* about keeping pigeons!'

'We do, Mum,' I said in a begging voice. 'Mr Duckins told us loads of stuff, didn't he, Garry?'

Garry rocked back on a kitchen stool. He smiled at Mum. She eyed him darkly. 'We know why he's got a star on his garage. It's so they recognize home when they've been in a race.'

'It's time you recognized home,' Mum said. 'If you stop any longer, *you'll* be on a perch in the shed.'

'Does that mean we can keep her then?' I

jumped in, hoping that if I kept on prodding, Mum would just stop resisting and crack.

'No,' said Mum, through tightly-pursed lips.

'Oh . . . fff!' I went, and banged the table with my fist. Mum gave me a look. She walked to the window and lowered the blind.

'Listen, Darryl.'

'Don't want to,' I mumbled. This was the first time Dad had spoken. All the while I'd been explaining things to Mum he'd been sitting at the table with a pen between his teeth, tapping away at his laptop computer.

'What you did for the bird was very heroic, but there has to be a limit to how far you can go. Mr Duckins is an expert, so take his advice. Look at the practical side of things. The bird is used to a life of racing. How's she going to be cooped up on her own in a shed, with no other birds around her? Imagine how she'll feel looking up at the sky through a long piece of glass and knowing she could never be out there again.'

'You don't have glass in a pigeon loft,' said Garry.

Mum tutted and threw some spoons into a drawer.

'That's not the point,' Dad continued. 'In effect, you'd be sending her to prison – putting her away for a life sentence. If she could fly, it wouldn't be so bad.'

There was a pause – as if Dad sensed he'd made a mistake. Maybe he had. I leapt in quickly. 'Mr Duckins told us she *might* fly again.'

'Darryl, you're wasting your time,' said Mum.

But I was looking at Dad. I could see he was hesitant. It was now or never. I had to convince him. 'All I want to do is nurse her, Dad. When she starts to fly we'll let her go.'

'Darryl—'

'At least she'll be able to feed herself . . . and make a nest . . . and . . .'

'Darryl!' Dad rapped his knuckles on the table. 'You *can't* let her go. She's a homing pigeon. Once you give her a roost, you've got her for good.'

'Well YOU get rid of her then!' I shouted.

'Darryl! That's quite enough of that,' snapped Mum.

But it wasn't for me. I hadn't even started. I pushed my chair away from the table so the legs made a screeching noise on the floor. 'You wring her neck and pluck out her feathers and shove her in the oven! See if I care!'

'Darryl,' Mum stormed, 'go to your room!'

38

'I WILL!' I shouted, almost in tears. 'And I'm never *ever* coming out AGAIN!'

That promise lasted about five minutes. I was lying on my bed with my face in my pillow when I heard the sound of the kitchen door opening.

'Take care, Garry,' I heard Dad say. His voice sounded very distant and solemn. *Take care*? I thought. *Take care of what? Not my pigeon.* I rolled off the bed and crept out on to the landing, just as Mum came out of the kitchen.

'Well,' sighed Dad, 'now what do we do?' He flopped back against the stairway and folded his arms.

'He does as we've told him,' Mum said firmly, plucking at an eyelash in the long hall mirror. 'He either takes it back to this Duckins chap or he lets the bird take its chances in the wild.'

Dad hummed thoughtfully and clicked his tongue.

'We can't keep it, Tim,' Mum continued. 'We're not equipped for housing pigeons. Like you said, it's a prison sentence – for us, as well as the bird. Besides, you know what he's like. The novelty will wear off in less than a week.'

No it *won't*, I thought. Why did parents

always say that? Why didn't one of them understand?

'I don't know,' I heard Dad mutter. He walked up the hall with his hands in his pockets. 'I think he's genuine. I really think he wants it.'

Yes! I mouthed silently, clenching my fist. My dad. What a hero. Come on, Dad. Come on.

'Oh now you're being as soppy as he is,' said Mum, picking up a brush and stropping her hair. 'It's a pigeon, Tim. Not a hamster or a rabbit. It needs special care. Where on earth would you put it?'

Dad shrugged. 'Like he said, the shed. I'm sure it won't mind sharing with a few old cans of paint.'

'No.'

'Claire—'

'No.' Mum turned. 'For a start we've always said, "no pets". You give him that bird and two minutes later Natalie will be screaming she wants a kitten. Anyway, there's an even better reason why he shouldn't keep it . . .' Mum paused. Dad and I both held our breaths. 'I'm worried about his schoolwork lately.'

Schoolwork? I hadn't expected that. What did school have to do with anything? I picked up

Natalie's cuddly rabbit and gave its ear a nervous tug.

'Don't look at me like that,' Mum said sharply, as if it was me standing there in front of her. 'You heard Mr Tompkins at the parent teachers'. His concentration keeps wandering in class. He's daydreaming, slipping well behind in certain subjects.'

'All kids go through that,' Dad defended. 'I was the same when I was his age.'

Mum shook her hair back and turned her gaze upwards. I just pulled away from the banister in time. 'I'm telling you. If you let him have that pigeon, you'll only make things worse.'

'I'm sorry, I disagree,' said Dad.

I squeezed the toy rabbit tight to my chest. *Please, Dad, please. Make her say yes. I promise I'll try really hard at school. I'll always do my homework on time. I promise.*

'I think the bird will have the opposite effect. I think the commitment and the responsibility of caring for it will focus his mind, not fog it up. I'm not saying he'll whizz to the top of the class just because he's got a pigeon in the shed, but . . .'

'But what?'

'Well, it *is* unusual. Who knows, it might be the making of him? It'll give him something personal to cherish – and it'll keep him off the streets.'

There was silence a moment. The whole world seemed to be waiting for Mum. I could almost *hear* her eyebrows knitting. 'All right,' she conceded, 'on your head be it . . .'

Yes! I punched the air in triumph and plonked a kiss on the rabbit's nose!

CHAPTER SIX

It was about half an hour later that Dad came up to tell me the news. I guessed they'd kept me waiting so long to make me sweat for mouthing off at Mum. But what they'd really been doing was working out a plan – a set of conditions I had to stick to. I only found out when I went downstairs to say thanks to Mum. I gave her a massive kiss on the cheek and she just went, 'Hmm, someone's in a good mood. I hope your father's discussed this with you.' At that point, Dad slipped into the lounge.

'Sit down,' he said. 'We'll do this together.'

There was loads of stuff. First, they explained, the bird was my responsibility and mine alone. I had to feed her and keep her clean and healthy. If they ever suspected she was being neglected she went straight to Mr Duckins, no questions asked. I had to buy her food from my pocket-money as well. I winced a bit at that because I didn't know how much pigeon food cost. I get five pounds pocket-money every week and I'm always broke when Saturday comes around. Mr Duckins had given me a small bag of mixed grain to start me off. He'd told me she needed enough to fill an egg-cup, twice a day. I guessed I had about a week's supply. I made a note to go to the pet shop later.

The worst bit was all the stuff about school. They didn't say anything too direct. They went 'round the houses' as my gran likes to say. Things like, 'We don't want this hobby to interfere with your homework, Darryl' and 'Education is important, we hope you understand that'. I knew what they wanted to hear, of course: 'I promise I'll try double-extra hard at school from now on'. It made me squirm. School is hard enough as it is. Especially English with Mr Tompkins. It's so-oo boring. Anyway, Mum looked pleased enough. And that was that. I was told not to get so uppity in future – and then I was excused.

I rang Garry straight away.

He came round next morning as we were finishing breakfast.

'Excuse me, but did you actually *leave*?' Mum asked as he stepped into the kitchen and wiped his feet.

Garry gave her a peculiar look.

'I swear that boy sleeps in our garage,' Mum muttered, plonking dishes on to the drainer. Dad just smiled and went on picking horses from the paper.

Natalie said, 'I want to sleep in the garage as well.'

'Eat,' was all Mum said in reply. Natalie stuck out her lip and stirred her cornflakes.

'We're going to see the pigeon,' I announced to the kitchen. I picked my baseball cap off the worktop and motioned Garry to follow me to the garden.

'I want to see the pigeon,' Natalie piped up.

'Soon,' said Dad. 'Darryl and Garry have to clean the shed first.'

'What?' said Garry.

'Come on,' I said. I grabbed a handful of his sweatshirt and hauled him outside.

'It's one of the conditions,' I began to explain as we walked down the garden and stopped by the shed. I rubbed the window and peered inside. Cherokee's box was exactly where I'd left it, slap bang in the middle of the floor. I'd covered the top with a loose piece of cardboard and punched a few air holes in with a pencil. Mr Duckins had said we should keep her quiet for the first few days, try not to let her flap too much. It didn't look as if she'd done any flapping whatsoever. And suddenly, I had this horrible feeling. What if I lifted the cardboard this morning and she was cold and stiff and rolled on her side, one eye staring, claws turned up?

'What conditions?'

Garry's question brought me back to my senses. 'Things we have to do if we want to keep her.'

'You're the one who's keeping her,' he said, confused. 'Why do I have to clean your shed?'

'Because you're my friend and I'll be going on holiday some time, won't I?'

Garry still looked confused. 'You're going to take her to the seaside? Won't she get lost among all those gulls?'

'Never mind,' I sighed. 'Just wait there.'

I unlatched the shed door and brought Cherokee's box out on to the lawn. My hands were shaking as I lifted the lid. She was sitting in a corner, all huddled up. There was a messy streak of poo on the bottom of the box and a few rolled oats that she hadn't pecked up.

'Hello, bird,' said Garry, leaning over my shoulder. He 'cooed' a few times and clicked his tongue. 'What you gonna call her, then?' he asked.

'Dunno,' I answered, lowering the lid. I'd been thinking about that ever since we'd left Mr Duckins' house. Why didn't fanciers give their birds names? Perhaps it was because they had so many they wouldn't be able to remember them all. It seemed a bit mean, though, just giving them a number. A bit like being in the army or something. I'd decided my bird would definitely have a name. I just didn't know what it was going to be, then.

'Polly,' said Garry.

'Dumb,' I said.

'It's what they call parrots.'

'She's not a parrot.'

'Polly pigeon. Sounds all right. Pretty Polly pigeon. Here, Polly pigeon. Who's a pretty boy, then?'

'Not you,' I said. 'Let's do the shed.'

There wasn't very much to tidy at all. We started by taking everything out and piling it into a heap on the lawn. Garry nearly split the seat of his jeans when he tried to lift an old bag of building sand. We moved that and a bag of cement out together, then we took it in turns to get the lawnmower, some garden tools, Natalie's old pram (that Mum was going to grow flowers in one day), a reel of wire mesh, some music magazines, some weedkiller, a box of old wood bits, some rolled-up carpet, a big stack of plant pots and finally, a shelf-load of paint cans and brushes.

The only thing left was Dad's old workbench. 'That as well?' Garry said with a gulp. The workbench looked a pretty solid fixture.

To his relief I shook my head. 'I'm going to put her box on top of that. When my birthday comes round I'm going to ask Mum for a proper nesting box, just like the ones in Mr Duckins' loft.'

'I'm getting the Man United away strip for mine.'

'Boring,' I sniffed, trying not to sound envious. I grabbed the yard brush and thrust it at him.

While Garry was sweeping the floor of the shed, I got on and cleaned the window. The glass was covered in a film of dust that smudged and smeared as I rubbed it with a tissue. I thought about writing 'Darryl's Loft' in big arched letters, but I didn't think Mum would be pleased if she saw it. The frame of the window was worse than the glass. Little clumps of moss were growing in the corners and it seemed to be a graveyard for hundreds of flies. When Garry wasn't looking I brushed them to the floor. Then I forced the window open and left it on the latch.

As we were putting the stuff back in, Dad and Natalie came down the garden. Mum was just behind them with a basket of washing. She stopped to peg some out on the line.

'Not bad,' Dad said, admiring our handiwork. 'Neat and tidy, like a workshop should be. Where's the pigeon box going?'

'On the workbench,' I said.

'Oh yes?' said Dad. 'And suppose I want to do some D.I.Y?'

'Fff,' went Mum. 'That'll be the day.'

'What's D.I.Y., Daddy?' Natalie piped up.

'It's no good asking him,' said Mum.

'She has to be off the ground,' I explained, bringing the conversation back to pigeons.

49

'So the vermin don't get her,' Garry pointed out.

'VERMIN!' Mum squealed, dropping her pegs. 'We're not having vermin in our shed, Darryl.'

'What's vermins?' said Natalie.

'Mice,' I said. I saw Mum shudder.

'I like them,' said Natalie. 'I wonder if we've got any vermins in our shed?'

'She's weird,' Garry muttered. I couldn't disagree.

'It's only a precaution,' I explained to Dad. 'It's really to keep her away from damp.'

'It had better be,' said Dad. 'What's the window doing open?'

'Pigeons need lots of air,' said Garry.

I nodded and qualified the statement some more. 'Mr Duckins said to give her plenty of air but not to let her sit in a draught.'

Dad looked a bit perplexed. 'How's she going to manage that with the window on the latch? Anyway, what's to stop a cat getting in?'

I shuffled my feet and looked at the ground. 'We have to put mesh across the window,' I murmured.

'Oh, do we?' Dad said, putting his hands

on his hips. 'Nobody said anything about *that* yesterday.'

'I forgot, sorry.' It was true, I had. But since the subject was raised, I reminded Dad we had some mesh in the shed.

'All right,' he sighed, 'bring it out here. And the hammer, and the cutters, and a handful of nails.'

'Shall we open a paint can, too?' asked Garry. He flapped an irritated hand at Natalie. She had picked up a peg and was going for his sleeve.

'Punnt?' went Mum, biting on a sock.

'Mr Duckins' loft is painted in black and white stripes. So the pigeons can see it from a long way off.'

'I don't think so,' said Dad.

'I know so,' said Mum, removing the sock and shaking it out. 'I'm not having a humbug in the garden, thank you. And we're not having a star on the roof of it, either.'

I glanced at Dad. He gave me a 'that settles that' sort of look. I just nodded and went to get the mesh.

While we were cutting the mesh to size, Mum said, 'Have you thought of a name for this poor bird yet? I can't keep calling it "the pigeon" for ever.'

'I *wonder* what your name is?' Natalie said, lifting the cardboard and peering in the box. I grabbed her before she could peg a wing.

'How about *Feathers*?' Mum suggested.

'That's naff,' Garry muttered, hoping Mum wouldn't hear. But Mum's got ears like satellite dishes – and a scowl as black as space to match. 'And what's your bright suggestion, *Gareth*?'

That made Gazza squirm. He hates it if anyone calls him Gareth. 'Dunno,' he said, and stuffed his hands in his pockets.

'I want to play at Indimans,' Natalie said suddenly. I looked her way. She had a feather in her hand and was waving it about like a fireworks sparkler.

'Nat-tt!' I started, thinking she must have pinched it from the box.

'All right,' Dad said, putting a hand on my arm. 'She found it on the grass. Let her play if she wants to.'

'I'm an Indiman!' Natalie announced to Garry. 'I wonder if you're a . . . boy cow!'

'Push off,' he muttered as she pegged his jeans.

'What about an Indian name?' said Dad. 'You could call her *Flies like the Wind* or something.'

'She can't fly,' I said.

Dad scratched his head. 'Well, you know what I mean.'

'I *wonder* why the pigeon can't fly,' said Natalie, flapping her arms and running in figures of eight on the lawn.

'I wonder if you'll ever stop saying "I wonder",' Mum huffed. 'And don't do that, you'll make yourself sick.'

'Urrrgghh!' went Natalie.

'Charming,' said Dad.

'Wonderbirds . . .' said Garry, suddenly inspired. 'Call her *Wonderbird One*! You know like Thunderb—'

'No chance,' I said, cutting him off.

'I know.' Everybody looked at Mum. 'Name her after an Indian tribe.'

Dad nodded. 'That's a good idea. Lots to choose from: Hopi, Navajo, Blackfoot . . .'

'She's got *pink* feet,' said Garry.

'Whee!' went Natalie.

' . . . Sioux,' said Dad.

'Yes, *Sue*,' said Mum. 'That's a nice name. We very nearly called Natalie that. Natalie, will you STOP doing twirls.'

'I'm a wonderbirds,' said Natalie. 'I wonder, I wonder . . .'

Then I remembered a name from History.

'*Cherokee,*' I said. 'Isn't that the name of an Indian tribe?'

'Yes,' said Dad. 'Cherokee. That's good.'

'Wonderbirds!' said Natalie, spinning into Dad.

'*Cherokee the Wonderbird!*' Dad said loudly, catching Natalie and swinging her round. He lowered her with a bump then patted a hand across his mouth and started to whoop. He did a hopping dance up the garden path.

'Don't you make it rain,' said Mum, jerking a thumb at the line of washing.

'As if,' scoffed Garry. He glanced my way. 'I still like *Wonderbird One* the best.'

'It's *Cherokee.*' I said, kneeling by the box.

'Wonder,' Mum added. '*Cherokee Wonder.*'

'Cherokee *Wonder*?' Garry turned up his nose. 'Stupid,' he said.

But I liked it – and it stuck.

CHAPTER SEVEN

About three weeks after we'd named Cherokee
I got the chance to keep my promise about trying
harder at school.

One morning, in English, Mr Tompkins
boomed, 'Public speaking. That is going to be
our topic today.' He wrote it on the board in
capital letters and underlined it twice in yellow
chalk. 'What do I mean by public speaking?'

Melanie Warner shoved up her hand. 'It
means doing talks, sir.'

'Yes,' said Mr Tompkins. 'Doing talks. That's
exactly what it means. Giving a lecture or speech

of some kind. Who can you think of who gives a speech?'

'Mr Blundell,' Graham Wheeler groaned from the back. A few people sniggered. Mr Blundell is our Head. He gives a boring speech about something called 'morals' at quarter past nine every morning in assembly.

'Yes,' said Mr Tompkins, ignoring the laughter. He threw his chalk into the air and caught it again. 'Mr Blundell is a very able speaker. Who else? Come on, let's have some famous ones . . .'

So we had to reel off a great long list. Claire Parker said 'The Queen' and I said 'The Prime Minister'. Mr Tompkins said they were both very good. Garry said 'Ryan Giggs' and everybody laughed. Sean Forrester called him a total wally. Garry chucked a ruler but it hit Donna Glass. Donna threw it back and it hit Emma Green. Mr Tompkins threatened them all with detention.

'Anyway,' he went on, 'if we've all stopped lobbing missiles round the room the point is this: where did these people *learn* to make speeches?'

I knew what was coming. 'School,' he was going to say, any second now.

'School,' he said. I made a snoring noise and slipped down in my seat. 'They learned it in school. In their *English* lessons, to be precise . . .'

By now, everyone was doodling on their pads. Mr Tompkins was gliding between the desks, just like a lion stalking its prey. He tossed his chalk into the air again and snatched it back about an inch above my head.

'So.' The sharpness of the word made me squeeze my eyes shut. I opened them again when Mr Tompkins patted his hand on my shoulder and told me to sit up straight in my seat. 'How is it done, Darryl? How do we learn this remarkable gift?'

'What gift?' said Connor Dorley.

'Oration, Connor. The gift of oration.'

'Or what?' said Garry.

'*Or . . . ration*,' Mr Tompkins repeated, drawing his hand away from his mouth like a magician pulling out a stream of hankies. 'Well, Darryl?'

I swallowed hard and knitted my fingers together. 'Don't know, sir,' I mumbled. 'You just do it, I s'pose. You just stand up and . . . talk about something.'

'Anything?' Mr Tompkins pressed, drifting quietly back towards the front. He picked a

Space Wars figure out of Billy Dunkley's grasp and dropped it on his tray of confiscated items. 'If I asked you to talk about baking a cake, you could come up here and do it, could you?'

'I could,' I heard Annie Gardiner whisper. She poked me in the back. I just wanted to curl up and roll down a drain.

'No, sir.'

'Hmm,' Mr Tompkins murmured. He glanced through the window and tutted at something. It wasn't enough to stop him talking. 'So what *could* you give a public speech about, Darryl? What single thing do you know most about?'

For a second, I seemed to be lost in a dream. That foggy sort of state I get in sometimes when we have to do a test and my mind goes blank. Then, without thinking, a word popped out . . .

'Pigeons.'

'Pigeons?' Mr Tompkins set his shoulders back. He gave me one of his questioning looks as if I might be trying to wind him up. The rest of the class were too stunned to respond. I could tell they thought I *was* making it up. Everyone except Garry Taylor, of course.

'It's true,' he said proudly, folding his arms

and smirking at all the questioning faces. He grinned at me and then at Mr Tompkins. 'Me and Darryl know *loads* about pigeons, sir.'

And that's how we came to be doing our project. The point Mr Tompkins was making was this, the easiest way to learn public speaking was by giving a talk about something you were good at, or something you enjoyed, or a hobby you had.

'In Darryl's case, pigeon fancying apparently.'

'Coo-oo,' someone trilled from the back.

Mr Tompkins sighed. 'See me afterwards, Connor Dorley.'

Normally, I hate doing projects. But at least this time we could do it in pairs. Garry and I teamed up straight away. I didn't know at first how we were going to work it. Mr Tompkins said both members of a pair had to talk on their subject for at least five minutes, but they must present a different aspect of it.

On the way home I explained to Garry what I thought he meant. 'If I give a talk about looking after pigeons, you have to talk about racing them or something.'

'That's not fair,' Gazza protested. 'I don't know anything about racing pigeons.'

'We could always go and ask Mr Duckins,' I said.

Garry scuffed the toe of his shoe in the gutter. There was a pause while we turned down Great Elms Road. Then he came back meekly, 'Can't we do a project on football instead?'

I was just about ready to punch his arm when suddenly something caught my eye. It was in the window of a shop called *Spines*, a second-hand bookshop that we passed every day but that neither of us had ever bothered to look in before.

Garry scuffed to a halt and followed my gaze. 'Wow,' he gasped.

There, tacked up on to the glass, was a huge and slightly faded poster. 'The Anatomy of a Racing Pigeon' was its title. It showed a picture of a typical racing bird with annotations pointing out all its body parts. There were some brilliant diagrams of the pigeon skeleton and all sorts of insets about where pigeons came from and what breeds there were. I checked the price: 95p.

'I'm having that for the project,' said Garry, slipping his sports bag off his shoulder and digging about in his pockets for the cash.

'I saw it first,' I said, put out.

'Tough.' He flashed a pound coin at me. Before I could catch him, he'd dashed into the shop.

While he was gone I looked at the rest of the window display. There were loads of books about wild birds, all carefully arranged on little stands. There was nothing else about racing pigeons, nothing in a book at any rate. But on a board just behind the furthest row of books were three small watercolour paintings – all of pigeons. I was squinting at them, trying to read the name of the artist, when Garry came out and bopped me on the head with the rolled-up poster.

'These pictures are good.' I pointed at the paintings.

'Boring,' Garry sniffed and bopped me again.

I could see what he meant. The pictures were colourful and very lifelike, but they were portraits, really, like photographs of someone's favourite birds. I let myself imagine a painting of Cherokee on my bedroom wall, but I couldn't imagine paying the price. Twenty-nine pounds for a picture of a bird? At even half my pocket-money, that would take at least . . .

I jumped back in shock. As I'd turned away

from the window of *Spines*, trying to do twenty-nine pounds divided by two pounds fifty in my head, I'd collided with a group of older boys. They were wearing the grey and yellow ties of our uniform, but I didn't recognize any of them. I guessed they were fourth-formers. One of them was linking arms with a girl. Another one stubbed out a cigarette.

'Sorry,' I mumbled to the one I'd bumped into.

'You will be,' he said, 'if you try that again.' He had long black hair flowing over his collar and eyes like the points of a powerful magnet. I moved backwards a little, nearer to Garry.

'What's he carrying?' the girl piped up. All five faces turned to Garry. Garry, stupidly, tried to hide the poster behind his back.

'Nothing.'

'It's a poster,' said the boy with the cigarette packet. 'He's got a poster. I bet it's his favourite pop star, aah.'

'Let's have a look, then,' the girl said to Garry.

Garry started to tremble.

'You heard her. Unroll it,' said the boy I'd bumped into. There was ice in his voice. Garry shook his head, scared.

'Unroll it,' sneered the boy, lunging forward. His hand gripped Garry under the chin.

'Cuff him, Warren,' one of them laughed.

'Get off him!' I shouted, tugging Warren's arm. 'It's only a picture of a bird. Get off!'

Warren flung out his arm and bundled me aside. 'Bird?' he snarled, grabbing my tie. He trod on my toes and I squealed with pain.

'A pigeon,' I blurted, covering my head, sure at any second he was going to thump me. 'We have to do it for a project at school.'

Warren lifted his foot. I felt the flat of his hand press into my chest. The next thing I knew I was flying backwards. *Wham!* I hit the bookshop wall with a thump and crumpled to the ground in a sorry heap.

Suddenly, the bookshop door flew open and a frail old man with a goatee beard and a satin waistcoat appeared at my side. He didn't look any stronger than a blade of grass, but he wasn't afraid to speak his mind. 'Clear away, you lot! Go on! Hoppit!'

'Get lost, grandad,' somebody muttered.

'You watch your lip,' the old man threatened. 'Another ten seconds and I ring the law.'

But Warren and his gang didn't care about the law. They gestured rudely with fingers and hands and sidled off up Great Elms Road, flapping their arms and doing impressions of pigeons cooing. As they crossed the road I heard Warren howl. 'Useless!' he cried. 'Not even close.' Before anyone could try again a bus pulled up and they sprinted for it.

'Good riddance,' the man from the bookshop muttered. Together, he and Garry helped me back to my feet. 'You all right, son?' he said, dusting my shoulders. I nodded. The old man looked relieved. 'You should try and steer clear of thugs like that. He's a nasty bit of work that one with the hair.'

'Do you know him?' asked Garry.

'Oh yes,' replied the man, gritting his teeth. 'Spigott, his name is. Warren Spigott.'

'Spigott!' Garry's mouth fell open in shock. He looked more scared than he had before.

The old bookseller hummed to himself. 'The shame of it is, if you knew his father you'd never believe he could spawn such a lout.'

But we could. We knew all about Lenny Spigott. The unkind, unthoughtful, uncaring man who liked to wring the necks of helpless birds. Lenny and Warren: like father, like son. I clenched my fists and turned my face towards

Great Elms Road. Warren's gang had boarded the single-decker bus and were shuffling along it like bubbles through a pipe. It pulled away as they found their seats – and disappeared up the Barrowmoor Road.

CHAPTER EIGHT

'I thought he was going to kill you,' said Garry as we stepped into the kitchen and banged the door shut.

I glanced up the hall. The door to the lounge was slightly open, the sound of the television leaking through it. 'Don't say anything to Mum,' I whispered. 'If she finds out we got picked on by Warren Spigott she'll be down to Mr Blundell and then we'll be for it because everyone at school will think we're cissies.'

'Don't care, he's bigger than us,' Garry

shuddered. 'What we gonna do if he comes looking for us in the playground?'

I grabbed two beakers off the drainer and made us each a drink of orange squash. It was just my luck to have Warren flipping Spigott going to our school. Double bad luck to get bullied by him. 'You'd better not tell about Cherokee, Gazza. If he finds out, he'll probably kill her himself.'

Garry sagged on a stool and sipped his squash. 'He can't get her now. She's yours. He'd be stealing.'

'Who'd be stealing?' Mum appeared from the shadows of the hall.

'No-one,' I said, trying not to sound too awkward. I turned to the cupboard to get a straw. I could feel Mum's gaze boring holes in my back.

'I should hope not,' she said, in a solemn sort of voice. 'If I thought either of you were involved in—'

'We're not stealing!' I shouted, turning quickly and slopping juice across the kitchen table.

Mum stared at me hard. 'All right,' she said, barely moving her lips. 'Now get a cloth, please, and clean up that mess.' She pointed at the juice. I sighed and grabbed a cloth.

'What's that?' she said as I moved the poster to wipe up the spill.

'We didn't steal it if that's what you think.'

Mum banged a hand down hard on the worktop. 'Don't you get sarky with me, young man. I asked a simple question, that's all.'

'It's a poster,' Garry said, drawing the heat. Mum obligingly turned his way. He picked the poster up and slid the rubber band off. Then he rolled it out like a tablecloth.

Mum blinked in surprise. 'Oh,' she said. She seemed a little disappointed that she hadn't uncovered some master plan.

'We have to do a project for English,' I explained, still in a rather sullen voice.

'About pigeons,' Garry added.

'Yes,' said Mum. 'Did you borrow this from the library, then?'

'We bought it,' said Garry. 'It's research, Mrs Otterwell.'

Even I blinked in surprise at that. I didn't know Garry knew words like 'research'.

'I see.' Mum ran a hand through her hair. 'Well . . . good,' she said approvingly. 'That's very . . . encouraging.'

'Thanks,' I muttered, just for something to say.

Mum cleared her throat and opened the freezer. 'We're having chicken drumsticks for tea tonight. They'll be ready in half an hour, OK?'

'Brilliant,' chirped Garry.

Mum immediately frowned. 'Don't your parents feed you at home?'

''Course,' he said 'We always have oven chips as well with drumsticks.' He drained his glass and jumped off the stool.

'We're going to feed Cherokee now,' I said.

'Fine,' Mum muttered into the recesses of the freezer. 'I suppose she'll be wanting oven chips as well . . .'

When we were safely out of earshot, Garry commented, 'She's weird, your mum.'

'She's all right,' I said. 'Except when she starts going on about school.'

Garry nodded sagely, as if he knew that situation only too well. Then his face brightened up and he changed the subject. 'Are we going to bring Cherokee out again tonight?'

I looked at the sky. It was slightly overcast but there wasn't even a hint of rain. For the last three nights I'd been bringing Cherokee out into the garden, encouraging her to settle in my lap and feeding her corn from the palm of my hand. She had grown a lot stronger since those first few days. There was a sparkle in her eye when she looked at her surroundings, and she could stand and walk like a normal bird, too. Once, daringly, I'd actually set her down on the lawn. She'd pottered around for nearly a minute until Mr Simmons next door had made a noise. Then she had squatted and spread her wings as if she was ready to spring into the sky. I'd panicked and snatched her up right away. I hadn't taken any more risks after that.

I unlatched the shed and went inside. Garry followed me in and stood in the doorway. He was muttering on about the poster and the project when I silenced him with a shocked gasp. Cherokee's box was not on the workbench. It had somehow tumbled off to one side and was lying wedged between the corner of the bench and the panelled wall of the shed itself. The flaps of the box were pointing downwards. I knew without looking she wasn't inside.

'Shut the door!' I shouted. 'And be careful where you're standing!'

'What?' he said.

'Gazza, shut the door!'

I pointed to the box. Garry recognized the danger and did as instructed.

Slowly I crouched down into the shadows. 'She's on the floor somewhere. She might be hurt. You check behind the mower; I'll look behind the workbench.'

For several minutes we searched in vain, crawling about on our hands and knees and poking our fingers into all the little places a pigeon might squeeze its hollow-boned body. We found nothing. Not a single feather.

'I don't get it,' said Garry after the second sweep. 'If she's not on the floor, where can she be?'

And then, suddenly, he did get it – though not in the way either of us expected. Something hit his arm with a moist splat. Instinctively, he put his hand out to feel it. 'Ugh,' he said, 'she's poohed on me!'

My heart nearly burst from the centre of my chest. I raised my eyes and the mystery was solved. We'd been looking for Cherokee in entirely the wrong place. She wasn't on the floor.

She was perched in the rafters.

CHAPTER NINE

I went tearing up the garden like a human comet, Garry trailing just behind.

'Steady on!' Dad complained as we burst into the kitchen. He was having his home-from-work clinch with Mum and looked a bit embarrassed, not to say annoyed, at the sudden explosion of noise.

'She can FLY!' I panted.

'Who can?' said Dad.

'Cherokee!' I clamoured. 'Cherokee can *fly*.'

Garry explained and displayed the evidence.

'Oh, that's going to please your mother,' Mum

wittered, and dragged him sleeve-first straight to the tap.

'I want to see Cherokee fly!' begged Natalie, trying to tug lumps out of Dad's best shirt.

'In a minute,' said Dad, patting her hand. 'How did she get from the box by herself?'

'Don't know,' I puffed. 'She just knocked it over. Unless . . . Nat! Have you been playing games in the shed?'

'I never,' she squealed, clutching Dad's leg.

Dad hugged her to him and frowned at me as if I ought to know better. 'Where's Cherokee now?'

'Still in the shed.'

'She didn't try to get away,' Garry piped up. 'She could easily have flown out over my head.'

'Stand still,' said Mum, yanking his arm.

'I never, I never, I never,' stamped Natalie.

'Hush,' Dad soothed her. 'Go watch the cartoons.' Natalie nodded and, pausing momentarily to stick her tongue out at me, skipped up the hall. Dad slipped off his jacket and hung it on the door. 'Well, she's obviously been feeling a bit confined. If she's flapped around enough to knock a fair-sized cardboard box off the workbench, she must be getting pretty frustrated in there.'

73

'Can't we get a *proper* box for her, Dad?' I bit my nails and glanced at Mum. She looked at Dad with her eyebrows raised.

Dad said, 'It's not the answer, Darryl. The bird is used to the open sky.'

'I'm not going to let her go!'

'Darryl,' Mum growled.

'You promised!' I shouted.

'Calm down,' said Dad, having a drink of water. 'Nobody said you have to let her go. But the situation's changed. We didn't anticipate this. I think you ought to give Mr Duckins a ring. Tell him what's happened and ask his advice. In the meantime . . .' he glanced at Garry's wetted arm, 'someone cover my mower with a sheet.'

'Fly?' said Alf as if he was surprised that any bird could be capable of it. 'How far's she gone?'

'Not far,' I mumbled and told him the story. A bellow of laughter rattled down the phone.

'So, she's a tough 'un after all,' he chortled. 'Spigott said she had plenty of grit.'

I ground my teeth at the mention of the Spigotts and moved him away from the subject fast. 'Is it wrong to keep her in a box, Mr Duckins – now that she can fly round properly, I mean?'

'Well, she'll be happier if she can come and go

as she pleases,'Alf grunted. 'How much room have you got in this shed?'

'Loads.'

'Well, then, get your dad to knock up a couple of perches and leave the box open during the day. You can give her a toss in the evenings for exercise.'

'Do what?' hissed Garry, contorting his head to try and get his ear a bit nearer the phone.

'You mean . . . ?' But I knew what Alf meant. I just didn't want to say it.

'Aye, five or ten minutes. Nothing too lively. Throw her up and let her have a little look around, then rattle the food tin and call her back.'

'But . . . ?' A twisting sensation of fear gripped my stomach. My fingers tightened around the phone.

Alf seemed to guess what was in my mind. 'She's a homing pigeon. She'll come back.'

I thanked Alf and rested the phone on the hook.

'Great!' exclaimed Garry, as perky as a prairie dog. 'Are you gonna do it? Are you gonna let her fly?'

'Don't know,' I muttered, looking down into my lap.

'Aw, come on-nn,' he pressed, curling his lip. 'It'll be brilliant – like having a remote-controlled plane.'

'Hmm,' I murmured. I was just as excited as he was really. But terror was blanking the feeling out. I kept hearing Mr Duckins' voice in my mind: *she's a homing pigeon. She'll come back.* That was the problem. I knew she'd come back. She was a Wonderbird. She had cheated death. But when I set her free, which home would she return to?

Our garden shed?

Or Lenny Spigott's loft?

CHAPTER TEN

'There – are – lots – of – different – types – of – pigeons. There – are – fancy – pigeons – and – racing – pigeons – and – feral – pigeons. The – one – that – Darryl – and – me – found – in – the – park – was – a – racing – pigeon . . .'

'Just – a – second – Garry,' Mr Tompkins mimicked. 'You – don't – have – to – do – it – in – such – a – robotic – voice.' He swung his legs off the desk and paced up the classroom, waving his hands around like an actor. 'Public speaking is a creative art. It's all about captivating your audience and convincing them of your point of view. At the end of the speech we should all want to share your enthusiasm for the subject. So put a little bit of passion into it. Make it clear to the class just how much you love these birds.'

'But I don't,' Garry said. 'I love football, sir.'

Everybody laughed.

'You know what I mean,' Mr Tompkins sighed.

Garry nodded and went back to his notes. 'Racing pigeons are very intelligent. They can find their way home from long distances, as far away as 500 miles, but nobody really knows how they do it. Some people think they have a magnet in their head. Some other people think they naver-naver . . .'

'Navigate,' Mr Tompkins prompted.

' . . . finding a path by the sun or the stars. During the First World War, pigeons were used to carry messages. My grandad told me that.'

Everybody laughed again. 'Shush,' said Mr Tompkins.

Garry went on. 'The pigeon is a very light bird. It only weighs a few hundred grams, but its wings are strong and capable of beating fast enough to carry it at speeds of up to 70 miles per hour.'

'That's faster than our car!' Connor Dorley piped up.

'Let him speak,' Mr Tompkins tutted. 'Go on, Garry. This is very interesting.'

Garry walked to the blackboard where we'd taped up the poster we'd bought in *Spines*. 'This is what a pigeon looks like inside.' He used a stick to point to a drawing of the skeleton. 'It has hollow bones which are very brittle. It has a big puffy bit at the front of its chest called a crop. This is a bit like a stomach. Pigeons eat hard food like maize and maple peas and wheat. They also eat grit.'

'Grit?' said Donna Barker, pulling a face. 'They eat bread in town.'

'My sister eats soil,' Graham Sweeton said.

'*My* sister eats coal,' Melanie Warner contested.

'You'll all be chewing the end of a pen if you don't be quiet,' Mr Tompkins warned. 'The next person to interrupt gets detention and an essay – all about birds. Now, tell us why pigeons eat grit, Garry.'

'They use it to mash up their food,' he answered. One or two people wrinkled their noses. Garry continued. 'They have lots of different types of feathers as well.' He pointed to the diagram. 'In the autumn, they all fall out and grow back again. This is called the moult.

'In conclusion . . .' (we all had to say that at the end of our speech) 'pigeons are interesting birds to keep. They are loyal to their owners and racing them can be a rewarding hobby. They live about fourteen years if they are looked after properly. That is what Darryl is going to talk about now.'

Garry blew a deep breath and stepped back from the desk.

'Excellent,' said Mr Tompkins. 'Short and sweet but very informative. Let's show our appreciation, class.' We all gave Garry a round of applause.

Then it was my turn. I stepped up to the front.

Like Garry, I'd written down in my workbook what I was supposed to be saying, but I soon discovered I didn't need it. I started off by telling everyone how we'd found Cherokee, and even how we'd come to name her. After that it all just seemed to tumble out naturally. When I got to the 'in conclusion' bit and finally finished off there was absolute silence. I looked at Mr Tompkins. He folded his arms and stared rigidly at me. I thought I'd done something wrong at first, but then he started to nod very slowly and said, 'Goodness, that *was* a passionate speech. Do you know you've been talking for fifteen minutes? And look at them, Darryl . . .' He swept out a hand. '. . . Your audience is *gripped*.'

'Gobsmacked, more like,' I heard Garry mutter. I flushed with pride and couldn't resist a smile. It was the first time I'd done really well in English.

When my thunderous round of applause had died down, hands began to pop up all over the room.

'One quick question each,' said Mr Tompkins. 'Or we'll all be here till this time next week. Over to you, Darryl.'

'Thanks, sir,' I said, and beckoned Garry back.

The first question came from Jennifer Quigley. 'You know when you said you have to pay for Cherokee's food yourself? How much does it cost?'

'Pigeon mix from the pet shop is 27p a pound,' I said.

'She eats about an ounce a day,' Garry added.

'And there are sixteen ounces in a pound,' I continued.

'So it costs?' said Mr Tompkins. We fumbled with the sum.

'About 2p a day,' I offered rather quietly.

'That's right,' said Mr Tompkins. 'Next question. Ryan?'

I beamed at Ryan Harvey. This was brilliant. I wished Mum and Dad could be here to see it.

'When she could fly and you let her out of the shed the first time,' Ryan asked, 'weren't you afraid she might fly away?'

I got a lump in my throat when I thought about that. My mind pitched back to the night we'd come home and found Cherokee sitting up in the rafters. It had taken me ages to gather the courage to let her go in the open air. *Please don't fly to Lenny Spigott*, I'd begged her. *This is your home. Please come back.* Before releasing her I'd looked towards the house. Mum, Dad, Natalie and Garry were all there, watching from the upstairs windows. I lifted Cherokee up to the sky. She cocked her head at the passing clouds, her dark-blue neck-feathers ruffling in the breeze. I could feel the beat of her heart in my hands and her warm toes scratching against my skin. I waited for an upward gust of wind and then, slowly, I parted my hands. *Fly*, I whispered. *Cherokee! Fly!* And she was gone, wings hammering like helicopter blades as she dipped across the garden in a low-flying arc that ended in a stumble on top of the dustbin. For a moment, I thought that was all she would do. And I wanted to pound across the garden and grab her, afraid the exertion had been too much. But she was tough, like Mr Duckins had said. As I turned, she put her head back and stretched, and suddenly she was clattering upwards, vertically upwards, straight to the roof. She landed briefly on the smooth grey slates, then fluttered higher still – to the TV aerial. It shook and wobbled under the impact. I ran into the shed to fetch my tin. By the time I'd come out again, Cherokee was gone.

'Darryl?' Mr Tompkins' steady voice prompted.

'Sir?'

'Are you with us? Ryan wants to know if you were frightened you'd lose Cherokee Wonder on her maiden flight?'

I stared at Ryan. He had his chin on his palms and was giving me the knitted eyebrows look. 'Yes,' I confessed. 'Dead frightened.'

'So was I,' said Garry, looking serious. 'I thought she'd gone to Barrowmoor.'

'Why Barrowmoor?' Mr Tompkins asked.

I gave Garry a kick on the back of his ankle. We'd made a deal that we wouldn't mention where Cherokee had come from, and so far nobody had bothered to ask.

'Er . . . dunno,' Garry shrugged. 'She just went that way. She came back, though,' he added, with a toothy grin. 'She only flew round and round the sky. Darryl got her in by shaking the food tin.'

Mr Tompkins smiled. 'I expect that was a special moment, Darryl?'

'Yes, sir,' I muttered. I didn't dare say I'd cried. But I had. I'd sat in the shed for ages afterwards and wept so much there was a puddle on the boards.

'Anyway,' Mr Tompkins said, craning his neck and glancing at the clock, 'time is slipping away from us fast. We've only ten minutes before the bell. I'm afraid you'll have to ask Darryl and Garry the rest of your questions out of school.'

'Aw, sir!' everyone groaned at once. 'We can do loads of questions in ten minutes, sir!'

'True,' said Mr Tompkins, 'but I've saved this time for something rather special. You won't complain when you know what it is.'

The room buzzed with muttered words. Mr Tompkins winked at me. I went into the cupboard behind his desk and came out carrying a cardboard box. It was a box my Auntie Julie had used for taking her cat to the vet in once. But there wasn't a cat inside today.

The gasp when I lifted Cherokee out was almost loud enough to rattle the windows.

'Nobody move!' Mr Tompkins bellowed as twenty-four kids pressed forward in their seats. 'Darryl will carry her round the room. If you're gentle, he says you may stroke her.'

And everybody did.

It didn't stop when class had finished either. The whole school seemed to know we had a pigeon and loads of people wanted to see her. Garry said we should have charged 10p a look. We made our way to the gates that night like rock stars going through a crowd of fans. And it was outside the gates that something happened. I was waiting for Garry to stop showing off to Christine Thompson and come back with the cat-box so I could put Cherokee in it, when a finger tapped my shoulder and a squirmy voice said, 'Pleeze, Darryl, can *I* see your birdie?'

I knew that voice. And it wasn't really squirmy. I turned in fear. It was Warren Spigott.

'Let's have it, then,' he said harshly. He was with two others: the girl we'd seen before, and a ginger-haired boy in blue sunglasses.

I shook my head and held Cherokee close. She struggled as if she realized something was wrong. 'She's tired,' I said.

'Don't get smart with me,' said Warren, hooking two fingers inside my collar. I tried to pull away but he tightened his grip.

'Come on,' said the girl. 'This is boring.'

Warren ignored her. 'Let me hold her,' he demanded. He flicked one finger under my chin. It didn't hurt much but it made me grimace. The boy in the sunglasses snorted a laugh.

'It's all right,' said Warren, dead close to my face. 'I know about birds. She'll be safe with me.'

'No,' I said sharply, looking round for Garry. Where was he when I needed him most?

Just then I felt a searing pain in my ear. The boy in the glasses had grabbed my lobe and was starting to pinch it between his fingers.

'Get off!' I yelled.

'I'm only doing your blackheads,' he sniffed – and pinched a bit harder.

That was all I could take. I screamed again and let Cherokee go. I thought if I could throw her into the sky she would home to the shed and it would all be over. She would be safer in the sky than in the hands of Warren Spigott.

But she didn't make it into the sky.

As I moved to let her go Warren guessed what I was doing. It was just like a nightmare relay race. She flapped her wings twice and went out of my hands, fluttering madly, straight into his.

'Got you,' he said.

'NO!' I shouted. I flailed a leg and tried to kick him. The boy in the glasses got me in a bear hug.

'Hmm,' went Warren, 'what do you reckon, Paula?' He pushed Cherokee close to Paula's face.

'*Please*,' she complained, turning up her nose. 'Come on, let's go. Let the squirt have his stupid bird.'

Warren just smirked. He folded Cherokee into his hands and held her the way Mr Duckins had taught me. 'Which club you in?' he said, looking at her closely.

'Let her go,' I said. 'Just let her go.'

'She's a racer,' said Warren. 'Where'd you get her?' He turned her up and examined her ring.

'She's mine,' I said bitterly. 'Leave her alone.' I struggled with the arms around my chest, wincing as a knee drove into my back.

'I've seen this bird before,' said Warren.

'Let her go!' I cried, tears welling in my eyes. 'Let her go. I saved her! She's mine! Let her go!'

There was a movement of feathers. 'Hold up,'

said Warren. He had Cherokee's wing extended now. I knew he was looking at the code underneath.

Suddenly Paula tapped her foot on the ground. 'Tompkins,' she hissed. 'Sean, let him go.'

The arms around my chest whisked away like snakes. I stumbled almost breathless to the ground. Warren and his mates went into a huddle.

'Right, what's going on here?' said Mr Tompkins, approaching at a brisk, accelerated march. Garry was tucked in close behind. So that's where he'd been – to fetch Mr Tompkins.

'Just looking at the bird, Mr Tompkins,' said Warren. He was holding Cherokee properly now, innocently stroking her neck with his thumb.

Mr Tompkins flashed a glance at me. I tried not to let him see my face. 'Give it back, Spigott, and get on your way.'

'I know about birds,' Warren Spigott sniffed. 'Shall I tell you about their markings, Mr Tompkins?'

Mr Tompkins opened the front of his jacket and put his hands very firmly on his hips. His voice dropped to a dangerous growl. 'I won't tell you again, Spigott. Give the bird back.'

'To its rightful owner, you mean, sir?'

'GIVE IT!' Mr Tompkins thundered. He thrust an angry finger in my direction.

Warren Spigott responded with a spiteful grin. He held Cherokee out and I took her from him. Garry opened the box and I put her inside.

'Now go,' Mr Tompkins ordered them. 'Before I put you in detention for the rest of the month.'

Warren flicked his unwashed hair off his shoulder. He stuffed his hands really deep in his pockets and backed off slowly, whistling as he went. He didn't say a word but I could read his eyes. *I'll see you*, he was saying.

I'll sort you out – thief.

CHAPTER ELEVEN

'Barbed wire,' said Garry. 'That's what we need. Barbed wire round the shed and a line of broken glass in front of it. Like they do on the industrial estate. He wouldn't be able to get near her then. Or one of those infra-red detector sort of gadgets that bleep like mad if you walk through the beam. No, I know! We could dig a big hole right near the shed door and cover it with branches like they do when they're catching tigers in the jungle! It'd be ace. When he steps on the branches . . . poom! He falls into a pit and gets eaten alive by Spigott-eating . . . spiders! Or snakes! Or snails! Or . . .'

'Gazza?'

'What?'

'Nothing,' I sighed. I flopped back on my bed and stared at the luminescent shapes on the ceiling: rockets, moons, planets, stars. I wished I could be lost in space right then.

I'd been a little lost ever since we'd got home. After the quietest tea in living memory (according to Mum) we'd gone to my room to listen to some music. Well, that was the theory; the stereo was on, but we weren't really listening. Garry had his nose in a football book and I'd found a tennis ball to bounce off the wall. After twenty-seven minutes of hitting Alan Shearer in the belly-button, I'd finally cracked and lobbed the ball into a pile of dirty washing.

'I hate Warren Spigott,' I muttered beneath my breath. It wasn't supposed to be loud enough for anyone to hear, but Garry was on edge and could have heard a flea sneeze. No sooner had the words come through my lips than he'd started on his methods of defending Cherokee from surprise attacks by the Spigott gang.

'Geese!' he cried, eyes aglow. 'Guard geese'd be *brilliant*! Connor Dorley said he got chased by some once when he was metal-detecting on Goodmud's farm.'

'Don't be pathetic. We can't get *geese*.'

'Hmm, s'pose not,' Garry conceded. 'They wouldn't be much use if he came in a fork-lift truck and tried to steal the whole shed with Cherokee in it, anyway.'

I threw a T-shirt at him. 'He's not going to try and steal her, stupid. All he has to do is tell his dad we're keeping her. Then Lenny Spigott will come round here and start a big argument and I'll have to give Cherokee back and Mum'll go mad and say I'm never to have a pigeon again – EVER. That's what's gonna happen. I *hate* Warren Spigott. I hate him! I hate him! I—'

'Darryl?' There was a rapid knocking on the door.

I blinked at Garry. He reached out and opened it.

'Turn that down,' Mum said sharply, jerking a thumb at the music system. Garry tweaked the remote. Mum looked across at me. 'Don't lie on your bed in your trainers, Darryl. Come on downstairs – there's a phone call for you.'

'Phone call?' I propped myself up on my elbows.

'That's what I said. Trainers – off.'

I swung my feet off the end of the bed. Garry hadn't moved. His eyes were like moons. 'Who is it?' he hissed.

'How should I know?' Mum shrugged. 'Some boy from school. That's all he said.'

'School?'

'Yes – school.'

'*Our* school?' I asked.

Mum shook her head in exasperation, 'No, now I recall he said he was from Eton. Come on-nn.'

Garry bit his lip. 'How old was he?'

'I don't know!' Mum spluttered impatiently. 'I expect he's one of your barmy classmates, which would make him officially twelve years old with a mental age of three. Now will one of you come downstairs and answer this call. The poor boy's bill must be astronomic.'

'Did he sound . . . friendly?' Garry persisted.

Mum glared at me. 'I'm going,' I said.

I felt like cutting the wires as I walked to the phone. Or yanking them from the socket like you see in films. I was certain the caller was Warren Spigott. Or Lenny Spigott. Or Mr Tompkins saying, 'Darryl, I want to hear the truth about this pigeon . . .' Or the police. My heart went wallop. What if it was the police?

What if they came and drove me away in a panda car and locked me in a cell and would only feed me on bread and water until I confessed to thieving a prized racing pigeon?

I picked up the phone.

'Is that Darryl?' said a voice.

'Might be,' I mumbled.

The caller paused, confused. 'Is it Garry, then?'

'No.'

The caller paused again. 'Is it . . . 541-2351?'

I glanced at our number. 'Who wants to know?'

'Ryan.'

'Ryan who?'

'Ryan Harvey – from school. Come on, Darryl. Stop messing about.'

I allowed myself a gulp. 'Sorry, I thought you were someone else.'

'Who?'

' . . . Dunno.'

Ryan tutted hard.

'What do you want?' I asked.

'Nothing,' he grumbled. 'It doesn't matter. I just wondered if I could come and see your pigeon flying, that's all . . .' He put down the phone.

I was like that all weekend – a real bag of nerves. Every time the phone rang, I hid somewhere. When the doorbell buzzed, I bolted for the loo. It was terrible, waiting for the moment to arrive – the moment when Warren would come and sort me out. Or send his dad round. Or do *something* horrible. But it didn't happen then. Not that weekend. Not Monday even. I'd almost forgotten about Warren Spigott by the time I did run into him again.

When I did, it was outside the papershop near *Spines*. I was reading Garry a useless joke off a lollipop stick when I realized he wasn't listening to me. His face was ashen, his gaze lost somewhere over my shoulder. I knew before I turned what I was going to see.

'You,' said Warren Spigott. He beckoned me to him. It was just him and the ginger-haired boy this time.

'What?' I said.

'Come here,' he snarled.

I inched a bit closer, near enough to smell his breath.

'I've been looking through my old man's records,' he said. 'And guess what I found?'

I gave a silent shrug.

'Guess,' he growled.

'Don't know,' I muttered. I hunched my shoulders and started to quiver.

'Don't know,' he mimicked. The ginger boy laughed. Suddenly, Warren's hand was under my chin. He tipped my face up so I had to see his eyes. 'That bird,' he spat, 'was a winner once. Placed first in a hundred-mile sprint, she was. She's valuable, that bird. She was one of Dad's favourites.'

'No she wasn't!' I blurted. 'He was going to kill her!'

Warren grabbed my tie and wrapped it round his fist. 'Why would he kill a bird like that?'

'Her wing was broken!' Garry piped up.

'Shut it!' snapped Warren. 'I'm asking him.' He shook me so hard my pen fell from my pocket. 'Does she fly?' he growled.

I kept my mouth shut.

'Well?' roared Warren, winding up his grip. He stretched me on to tiptoes and I started to gag.

'Yes!' squealed Garry. 'She flies! Let him go!'

There was silence a moment. Warren glared at my face then shoved me away. 'You thieved her,' he sneered.

'Didn't,' I coughed.

'Yeah, you did,' he said. 'Took her away

under false pretences. My dad's the rightful owner of that bird. And you know what I think?'

I shook my head.

'I think if he knew she could fly again, he'd want her back. I'm gonna tell him where she is . . .'

'No!' I shouted.

'She's ours!' hailed Garry.

'Butt out, you! I haven't finished.' Warren looked around and bit the side of his thumb. 'I'm gonna tell him everything I know – unless . . .'

'Unless what?' I gulped.

Warren's dark eyes narrowed. He grabbed me again and our noses touched. 'Unless . . . you become my *slave*,' he whispered.

'S-slave?'

He nodded and made our foreheads clunk. 'You do as I say. You get what I want, or the bird . . .' He made a squawking noise. I closed my eyes and a tear ran out. 'Understand me, squirt?'

'Yes,' I sobbed.

'Good,' said Warren, grinning at Ginger. He straightened his cuffs and pushed me away. 'See you around then – *slave*.'

CHAPTER TWELVE

'Have you noticed anything strange about Darryl, lately?'

I froze in my tracks. It was ten o'clock at night. I was sneaking downstairs for a chocolate biscuit when I heard Mum's voice through the front-room door.

'He was wearing odd socks yesterday,' Dad said, almost drowned out by the TV news. I crept up and pressed my ear to the door.

'That's normal,' Mum laughed. 'I mean strange as in . . . distant. I've been noticing it now for the past couple of weeks. He seems a bit . . .

I don't know, *lost* in himself. As if there might be something he can't work out. I can't put my finger on it, but there's something wrong. I know there is.'

I squeezed my eyes shut and raised my fist to my mouth, biting hard on the side of my finger like cowboys bite bullets when they're having an arrow pulled out of their chest. I had an arrow in my chest as well. It was called Warren Spigott, but I couldn't pull it out.

'Well it can't be school,' I heard Dad say, 'if what Mr Tompkins told you is right.'

I could almost see Mum's eyebrows knitting. I listened hard, hoping I'd hear what Mr Tompkins had said.

'Suppose not,' Mum murmured. 'He was gushing with praise about that pigeon project. I don't know. Darryl . . . he's just not *responding* properly. Do you know what I mean? He's wandering around in a trance some days. And he spends such a lot of time in the garden at the moment. Come the winter, he's going to freeze into a gnome.'

Dad chuckled. The TV went dead with a gentle *poom*. The silence seemed to bring Dad closer to the door.

'You can't say he isn't looking after the bird.

He's devoted to it. It's changed his life.'

'Yes,' Mum agreed. 'But how? That's the problem.' She let out a sigh. 'I'm telling you, Tim. I know that boy. Something isn't right with him.'

Dad clicked his tongue. The settee creaked as he sank back into it. 'Well, all we can do is keep an eye on things. If there is a problem, we'll spot it soon enough. He'll perk up when you've taken him to Weaver's.'

Weaver's? I pulled away from the door. What was *Weaver's*? It sounded horribly like a dentist or a doctor.

'I hope so,' Mum said. 'It should be quite an experience. I've never been to a basket works before.'

A *basket* works? What was going on? I felt uncomfortably like a cat that was being told it was off to the V-E-T's for a snip.

'By the way,' Mum added, as I was about to tiptoe back to my room to look up 'basket works' in my school dictionary, 'did you have five pounds from my bag this morning?'

I froze dead on my toes.

'Not guilty,' said Dad in a tone of clear denial. 'I had a couple of quid from the phone tin at the weekend. Nothing from your purse.'

'Umm,' Mum went. 'I must be going dotty. I was sure I had three fivers in my change from *Shopwise*.'

'You could have dropped one?' Dad suggested. 'It's easily done.'

'Hmm,' Mum muttered. But I could tell she wasn't sure. I knew my mum. She was like a detective. There would be all sorts of things going through her mind. I just hoped she didn't come to the right conclusion – and make me turn out my pockets in the morning . . .

I'd never stolen anything from Mum and Dad before. But I had to have the money – to pay Warren Spigott. As I crept back up to my room that night, half of me kept wanting to turn right around and bolt into the lounge and throw myself into Mum's arms and cry, *It was me, Mum. It was me. I'm sorry. It's because . . . It's because . . .*

But that was it. How could I tell her it was because of Warren Spigott? If I did, he'd win and Cherokee would have to go back to Barrowmoor. I couldn't lose her now. I just couldn't. I loved her. She was *my* bird. She *was* – and I'd been forced to steal from my parents to prove it.

At first it hadn't been so bad with Warren. He'd made me run errands, just stupid things like: *Go and unlock Paula's bike and wheel it to the front gates. Take this book back to the school library. Polish my shoes. Hold this mirror while I comb my hair, slave.*

Then one day, it changed. I was playing football with Garry at break-time when Warren whistled. He had what he called his 'slave' whistle. It was so loud you could hear it all over the school. When I heard that whistle I was supposed to run to him. I got a Chinese burn if I wasn't at his side within a minute.

That day, the day he turned me into a thief, I made it in time to the back of the bike sheds.

'Close,' he sneered. I put my head down and frowned. I was easily twenty seconds inside the minute. I walked up to him and bowed.

'You called, sir.' I got a punch if I didn't do that.

'See this,' he sniffed. I raised my eyes. He squashed a Coke can flat in one hand. 'Put it in the bin and get me another.'

'Another squashed one?' I said.

'Cheeky sod,' said Ginger, blowing smoke into the air.

Warren's face turned dark. 'Don't get smart

or you'll regret it, squirt. Get me a full one.'

'Crisps, too,' Ginger added.

'Yeah, crisps,' Warren nodded. 'Well, go on. What you waiting for?'

I hardly dared say it. But I had to. I was broke. 'Money,' I whispered, and opened my palm.

Warren filled it with pain, slapping his clenched fist hard across my fingers. Then he went for my head, but I ducked that one. 'You know what, squirt? My dad was only saying about that bird last night. "I wish I still had that pied hen," he said. I was almost tempted. Do you know what I mean?'

'Yes,' I said. I knew what he meant. And I knew he was lying, but I couldn't afford to take any risks.

I couldn't afford the pop or the crisps or the magazines or the sweets or the bus fares or the cigarettes he'd made me buy for several weeks either.

So I'd borrowed from Garry.

Or the phone.

Or Mum's purse.

And Mum was right: I did feel lost – and sick, and ashamed. I didn't know where it was going to end. Every morning when I woke I thought about it. I felt like I was going barmy.

Garry sort of agreed when I rang him secretly on the Saturday morning that Mum was taking me to the basket works.

'Perhaps it's where they take basket cases,' he hissed. 'You know, nutters – loony people.'

'Thanks a bunch,' I said and slammed down the phone.

In the car, on the way, Mum was surprisingly bright. 'Cheer up-p,' she said. 'You'll like this, it's a treat.' She took her hand off the wheel and ruffled my hair.

Some treat. I was going to a child psychiatrist or something. I folded my arms and stuck my head in my chest. 'Where are Dad and Natalie, then?'

Mum sighed and shook her head. 'Honestly,' she griped, 'you're so suspicious. This is my way of treating you for trying so hard at school just lately.'

I blinked, confused.

Mum went on, 'Your Grandma Thornton won forty pounds on the lottery last week. She's given twenty to you and twenty to Natalie.'

I jumped in my seat. Twenty pounds! It was the lifeline I needed to pay off my debts. 'Can I have it now, Mum?'

'Not so fast.' The car rolled up to a set of traffic

lights. Mum glanced at me and smiled. 'Your grandma was very interested to hear about Cherokee Wonder. I didn't know before but your Grandad Thornton kept pigeons once. Grandma thought it would be appropriate if this twenty pounds was to go towards Cherokee—'

'But—?'

'—which is why we're going to Weaver's Basket Works.'

I snorted rudely and flopped into my seat. 'What's a basket works?' I snapped.

'This,' said Mum, taking a sharp left on to an industrial estate and then left again on to an open forecourt.

I looked up. In front of us was a large open warehouse. Above it was a hand-painted sign with a daft cartoon of a pigeon's head. A speech bubble was coming from the pigeon's mouth.

Coo, Weaver's! Fancy that! it said.

CHAPTER THIRTEEN

'Well,' asked Mum, 'what do you think?' She unclipped her seat-belt and let it slide across her shoulder.

'Dunno,' I shrugged.

'Dunno,' she clucked. 'Is that the best you can do?' She rubbed an area of the windscreen clean with a tissue. 'You might try to show a bit more enthusiasm.' She leaned over and spoke as if sharing a secret. 'Apparently, you can get everything you've ever wanted for a pigeon in here.'

I stared at her blankly.

'Well you keep on saying that you want to get Cherokee a roosting box.'

'A nesting box.'

'All right, you're the expert – a nesting box.' She folded her arms and shrugged in dismay. 'Aren't you excited? I thought you'd be mad keen to root around in there.'

'I am,' I said, trying not to sound ungrateful. 'It's just . . . well . . .' I scratched a finger along the dashboard. 'Can't I get something else with the money?'

Mum sighed loudly and studied me hard. 'What is it with you at the moment, Darryl?'

'Nothing,' I mumbled, feeling uncomfortable under her glare.

'Is there anything you want to tell me? Because—' Suddenly, Mum was interrupted by a gentle tapping sound on her window. A red-faced man with wisps of grey hair clinging idly to his forehead was peering in. Mum wound her window down.

'Can I help you?' asked the man.

'Mr Weaver?' Mum prompted.

The red face nodded. 'What were you after?'

Mum reached over and ruffled my hair. I tutted in embarrassment and squirmed away. 'This is my son, Darryl,' she said. 'He'd like to buy a . . . *nesting* box if you have one.'

'Oh I think we can manage that,' said Mr Weaver. He stood up and dusted his hands on his overalls. 'Come into the warehouse and I'll show you the stock.'

Mum smiled and wound the window up. 'OK?' she said.

'Hmm,' I nodded.

'Cheer up,' she whispered, touching the back of her hand against my cheek.

'I'm all right,' I said, and slid out of the car.

As I closed the door Mr Weaver came to join me. He moved in bandy-legged foot-swinging steps, all the while whistling and wringing his hands. 'Don't recall seeing you before,' he said. 'Which club you with, lad? Barrowmoor? Spenner Hill?'

'I'm not in a club,' I replied a bit nervously.

'I think he's a wee bit young,' said Mum.

Mr Weaver stretched his head back and scratched his chin. 'I were thirteen when I joined my first club. The Nag's Head at Summerwell. Some grand flyers there. Grand pub, too.'

'He's definitely too young for *pubs*,' Mum added.

Mr Weaver raised an eyebrow but didn't reply.

He turned and we followed him into the warehouse, past row upon row of wooden palettes stacked high with bags of different kinds of pigeon food. I was about to ask why there were so many varieties when, without looking around, Mr Weaver spoke again: 'What size loft do you have, can I ask?'

'About six feet by ten,' Mum replied gaily. 'Just an average garden shed, I suppose.'

Mr Weaver shuffled to a halt. 'I meant, how many birds do you house in it?'

He turned to me for an answer. Mum nudged me to reply. My face burned hot. 'One,' I croaked.

'One?' Mr Weaver jerked in surprise. His brow resembled a freshly-ploughed field. 'Is it a racing bird?'

'Yes,' I answered.

'Her name's Cherokee,' said Mum.

I closed my eyes and took a short sharp breath. My muscles tightened to breaking point. If Mum had been Garry I'd have kicked her in the shins.

Mr Weaver responded with a puzzled nod. 'Right. You've got a racing hen . . .'

'Yes,' said Mum.

'Is she laying?'

'Is she what?'

Mr Weaver beat his chest and cleared some phlegm. 'I said, is she laying?'

For once, Mum stalled. I turned and read the label on a bag of grain.

Mr Weaver flapped his hands. 'Is she . . . y'know, with egg?'

'I sincerely hope not,' Mum said darkly. She flashed me a very suspicious look.

'She's not laying,' I said. At least I didn't think so. Mr Duckins hadn't said anything about it.

Mr Weaver cleared his throat and set his shoulders straight. A faraway look came into his eyes. 'So, let me get this straight, you have a single hen that isn't paired to a cock – and she definitely isn't laying?'

Mum nudged me again. 'Yes,' I said.

Mr Weaver frowned. 'Then why are you buying her a *nesting* box?'

That was it for Mum. 'Oh,' she said, changing the subject entirely, 'those paintings over there are very good. Do you mind if I have a look?' And without another word, she glided towards them.

They were hanging on a wall beside a brick-built office, twenty or thirty pictures of pigeons.

They were just like the ones I'd seen in *Spines*. But these weren't all of single pigeons. There were some of old men holding birds and another of pigeons feeding from a trough. The best was one of a bird in flight, coming back to a loft after being in a race.

'Local artist,' Mr Weaver said. 'Very popular around these parts. Knows everything there is to know about pigeons. Does this in his spare time, I believe. If you wanted a portrait of this hen of yours, I can give you his number and you can arrange a sitting.'

'Oh, I don't think we're in the market for a portrait,' said Mum. 'But I'd like to have a browse, if that's all right?'

'Be my guest,' Mr Weaver shrugged.

Mum seemed relieved. 'Perhaps you could show Darryl your range of boxes? It doesn't have to be a box. A rabbit hutch will do.'

'Mu-um,' I groaned.

Mum ignored me and opened her purse. She handed Mr Weaver two ten pound notes. 'I'm afraid if they're any dearer than that we'll have to leave it till another day.'

Mr Weaver parted his lips. 'I think we can find a nice "hutch" for that.'

We left Mum looking at the pigeon paintings

and carried on towards the back of the ware-house. Mr Weaver led the way past a rack of metal shelves, laden with medicines and all kinds of bits. There were bath salts for pigeons, vitamin pills, worming tablets, pot eggs (I hadn't got a clue what they were for), cage fronts, drinkers, scrapers, something called loft powder, lots of disinfectants and loads of sprays for getting rid of lice. I was glad Mum wasn't along to see them.

As we reached the end of the row of shelves I suddenly got a whiff of freshly sawn wood. 'Watch your head,' said Mr Weaver, bending his. We stepped through a door and entered a workshop lit by a single unshaded bulb. On a bench in the centre was an unfinished nest box. Tools and screws and sandpaper bits lay scattered among piles of curly wood shavings. There was a sweet pong of resin in the air as well. It mingled with sawdust every time I took a breath.

'Here we are,' said Mr Weaver, showing me a huge stack of nesting boxes. 'Solid ply with removable fronts.' He knocked one with his knuckle. 'Hand-made by yours truly. Last you a lifetime. Fourteen quid.'

'Brilliant,' I said. I meant it, too. It was right

that Cherokee should have a proper box. Why should Warren Spigott deprive her of that? The only thing niggling at the back of my mind was what Mr Weaver had said about nesting, and pairing Cherokee up with a cock. As he lifted a box down, I asked him about it.

Mr Weaver didn't reply straight away. He slid the box on to the workbench and blew a layer of dust off the cage front. 'You've not been at the flying game long, have you, lad?' I shook my head. Mr Weaver smiled. 'Sit down,' he said and pointed to a stool. I cleared the stool of sawdust, and sat.

'What you need to do is join a club. You'd learn everything there is to know about the birds, then. Good hobby for a bright young lad. Can be very rewarding, too. Lot of money to be won in pigeon racing . . . Oh yes,' he continued, spotting my flicker of interest. 'The best man can lift upwards of ten thousand pounds over a favourable season.'

'Ten thousand pounds!'

Mr Weaver sanded one edge of the box. 'You're not in that league yet, son. Not with one hen at any rate. Mind you, there's nothing to stop you going for a couple of novice events. Most of the clubs fly a junior section. If your bird's any good you might notch up a prize. I think Barrowmoor have one up this Saturday.'

'How much?' I was on the edge of my seat. 'How much can I win?'

Mr Weaver shrugged. 'Thirty quid? Fifty? I'm not sure what the going rate is these days.'

But it sounded pretty good to me. 'What do I have to do?' I asked.

'I've told you,' he repeated, 'join a club. There's no other way to enter the races. As a junior, it wouldn't cost the earth. And you needn't worry about what your mum said – it's not much to do with pubs or Working Men's Clubs. A lot of pigeon folk gather at someone's house. Where do you live?'

I told him. He spread his hands.

'Barely a wingbeat from Barrowmoor. Some fine flying men – and women – up there. Len Spigott for one. Now if ever there was a genius with pigeons . . . I'm sure Lenny'd be pleased to help you out. I'll give you his address when we're back at the office.'

'No!'

Mr Weaver railed back slightly. 'But I thought . . . ? A minute ago you were all for doing it?'

I was – but not with Lenny Spigott. Lenny

Spigott. He seemed to be everywhere. 'I'd have to ask my mum,' I muttered quietly. It seemed the best excuse I could offer.

Mr Weaver hoisted the box off the bench. 'Don't worry,' he winked. 'I'll ask her for you.'

'No!' I said, even more firmly.

Mr Weaver frowned. 'Make your mind up,' he tutted. 'Do you want to fly this bird or not?'

'Yes, I mean . . . well . . .' I didn't know what to say. Then a thought struck me and I voiced it out loud. 'Do you know Alf Duckins?'

'Alf?' said Mr Weaver. 'Everyone knows Alf. Been at the sport for fifty years. Next to Len Spigott he's the best customer I've got. Why, do *you* know Alf?'

'Yes,' I said, 'he's my friend.'

'There you go, then,' Mr Weaver sniffed. 'Have a word with Alf about joining a club.'

'I will,' I said, ideas tumbling like mad through my mind. 'Erm, how much did you say I could win again . . . ?'

CHAPTER FOURTEEN

'Homework,' Mr Tompkins announced. He walked to the blackboard and started to wipe it. It was the opportunity I needed to look across at Garry and tap my wrist.

Garry checked his watch. 'Eight minutes,' he whispered. He held up nine, then seven, then finally eight fingers.

'YES, GARRY?' Mr Tompkins boomed.

Garry stiffened in his seat. 'Sir?' he said.

'Did you want to ask a question?'

'No, sir,' Garry answered.

'Did you want to be excused to go to the toilet?'

Janet Perrywell sniggered. 'No, sir,' said Garry.

'Then put your hands down, pick up your pen and write these words on a clean page of your workbook. That goes for all of you. Quickly, please.'

There was a rustle of paper and a lifting of pens. The chalk rattled and tapped against the blackboard. I glanced at Garry. He put out his arms and pretended he was flying like a racing pigeon.

'What you doing?' Connor Dorley hissed.

Garry swooped and dipped. 'Nearrgh . . .' he went.

'I won't tell you again,' Mr Tompkins rumbled, looking sternly over his shoulder. Garry shrank into his seat and picked up his pen. He started copying down the words from the board:

COURAGE
CHARITY
FOOLISHNESS
SYMPATHY
NEGLIGENCE
COMPASSION

'Now,' said Mr Tompkins, stepping back from the board and juggling two pieces of chalk in one hand, 'by next Monday I want you to look up each of these words in the dictionary, choose one that interests you, then write five hundred words to illustrate its meaning.'

There was a mild groan from the back of the room.

'Come on,' said Mr Tompkins. 'It's not that difficult. Let's say I picked CHARITY, for instance.' He ringed the word in yellow chalk. As he did so a paper dart landed on my desk. The words 'Cherokee Wonderbird' were written on its wings and there was a hopeless drawing of a pigeon's head at the tip. I grinned at Garry and spread my arms – just as Mr Tompkins turned from the board.

'Migrating somewhere for the winter, Darryl?'

Silence. My face turned red. 'No, sir,' I mumbled, lowering my arms.

Mr Tompkins glared at us all. 'The next person I catch larking about stays behind after class. Is that understood? Now, pay attention. Charity. Charity is not only about giving money to worthy causes. You can also give your time and help to other people. If you choose this word for your homework assignment you might, for instance, write about someone who does the shopping for their elderly neighbour.'

He turned to face the board again, drew a dash against the word CHARITY and started to write his example beside it. I quickly scribbled, 'How long now?' on a wing of the dart and threw it back at Garry. Bad move. To my horror the dart soared and curved in a beautiful arc before descending towards the front of the room and skimming the floor by Mr Tompkins' feet. There was a collective gasp. Mr Tompkins whipped round. Everyone had followed the flight of the dart but my eyes were the last to dip away. Guilt was written all over my face.

'See me afterwards, Darryl,' Mr Tompkins said.

'I take it this afternoon's little disturbance has something to do with your pigeon?' he started. He had the paper dart opened out on his desk and was smoothing the creases, examining the words.

'Yes, sir,' I muttered.

'Hmm,' he hummed. He leaned back in his chair and put his hands behind his head. 'So what is it that's so important about your pigeon that it prevents you from paying attention during my English lessons? It didn't entirely escape my notice that you and Garry were in a tearing hurry to be somewhere else as soon as the bell went.'

I lowered my gaze and shuffled my feet. 'We're going to see Mr Duckins, sir. We're going to ask about Cherokee being in a race.'

Mr Tompkins stared at the ceiling a moment. 'Is that all?'

I wasn't sure what he meant, so I said, 'We have to be at his house at half-past four . . . tonight,' I added as an afterthought.

Mr Tompkins nodded slightly. He rolled forward in his chair and tapped the desk. 'Listen to me, Darryl. There is a time for hobbies and a time for schoolwork, and the first should not interfere with the second.'

'No, sir.'

'No, sir,' he repeated sharply. 'It's become all too apparent over the past few weeks that *something* is getting in the way of your learning. I had hoped it wasn't this pigeon business, especially as you did so well with your project, but it seems as if I'm wrong, doesn't it? I've seen that "lost" look coming back into your eyes again and I don't like it, I don't like it at all.' He paused, inviting me to make a comment. I just picked my nails and wished he'd get on with it. I didn't want to miss the bus to Alf's. He'd told us he was playing a bowls match at five.

Mr Tompkins shook his head and scrunched up the dart. He lobbed it softly into the bin. 'A good command of English is a valuable aid in anyone's life.'

'Yes, sir,' I muttered. He'd told us that about a million times.

'It's very disappointing to watch a bright boy like you squandering his chances of a decent education by—'

Phreeep!

Suddenly, the telling off was interrupted by a shrill whistle. I froze in terror. It was Warren's whistle. I couldn't see him for the blind across Mr Tompkins' window. It didn't matter anyway. I was never going to find him within a minute.

Mr Tompkins frowned and parted the slats of the blind with his fingers. He scowled left and right through the gap. 'If I find the boy who keeps doing that,' he muttered, 'I shall make him dig a very big hole and bury that whistle right at the bottom.' He let the blinds close with an angry snap and turned back quicker than I thought he would. I jerked to attention and bit my lip. 'Do you know who's responsible for that?' he asked.

'No, sir,' I said, trying not to fidget.

Mr Tompkins narrowed his eyes. 'Are you sure?'

'Yes, sir.' The whistle went again. This time, Mr Tompkins didn't turn away. His gaze locked solidly on my face as if he was trying to read my mind through the skin and bones. 'All right,' he said quietly, 'off you go.'

'Thanks, sir,' I said and headed for the door.

'Oh – and Darryl?'

I turned.

'Don't forget the words.'

'Sir?'

'The LIST,' he said in exaggerated tones, thrusting a finger towards the board.

I looked at the words and realized I hadn't written them down. It didn't matter. I could copy them from Garry. 'Yes, sir,' I said. 'Can I go now, please?'

'I suppose so,' he sighed.

I bolted for the yard.

CHAPTER FIFTEEN

'Dazza, this way!'

As I burst out of the school doors and belted down the steps Garry grabbed me by the arm and swung me around the side of the building. He put a finger to his lips and gestured me into a crouching run. I soon discovered why. As we hurried down the side of the Science block and scurried between the staff cars parked along the drive, I saw Warren Spigott from the corner of my eye. He and Ginger and another boy and Paula were hanging round the bushes near the front school gates. Warren was beating the bushes with a stick. 'This way,' Garry whispered, changing direction and hugging the mesh of the tennis courts. At the corner of the courts he flapped me to stop. He stuck out his neck and checked we were safe, then: 'Quick,' he hissed, 'we've just got time!' And we sprinted for the spinney at the back of the playing fields. By now, I understood what he had in mind. We were making for the bus stop before the one at school. We got there just as the bus arrived, paid our fares and pounded upstairs to the seats at the front. My throat felt like a kettle coming to the boil. I flopped out on the seat and panted like a dog. I was proud of Garry. His escape route was brilliant. I just prayed the Spigott gang didn't get on the bus.

About two minutes later my prayers were answered. 'Yes,' Garry cried. 'Easy! Ea-sy!' I guessed from the gestures he was making through the window that Warren and his gang were still outside the school. I blew a sigh of relief and raised myself into a sitting position.

'Was he mad?'

Garry swivelled in his seat and planted his feet on the front of the bus. 'Steaming,' he nodded. 'What you gonna do?'

I lifted my shoulders as if it didn't matter. But

a cold, cold shiver was running down my spine. Warren Spigott didn't like to be ignored. The next time I had to answer his whistle he was bound to do something horrible for sure. I told Garry I didn't want to talk about it. We talked about racing Cherokee instead.

'Whatever you do,' I told him firmly as we jumped off the bus at St Wilfred's Road, 'don't say anything to Alf about prize-money. We don't want him to think we're doing it for that.'

'But we *are* doing it for that,' Garry muttered, perplexed.

'I know,' I said tetchily. 'Just don't say it.'

'You'd better split it with me if you win,' Garry huffed. 'Fifty-fifty. You promised, Dazza.'

I opened the gate to Mr Duckins' drive. 'I always keep my promises, don't I?'

'You still owe me your baseball cap,' he sniffed.

I pretended not to hear him and rang the bell. A few seconds later the door swung open. Alf appeared in a set of white flannels. He looked a bit strange without feathers sticking to him, but he was still just as grouchy as ever. 'Oh aye – you pair,' he greeted us. 'Come on. Come through. I thought you were turning up at half past the hour? I've a taxi booked for five o'clock. You'll have to be on your way by then.'

Garry glanced at his watch. 'Ten to five,' he hissed.

I clenched my fists. 'Sorry, Mr Duckins. The bus took ages.'

'Aye, well,' Alf grunted and walked on through to the back of the house. He stopped at the table by the patio doors and packed a towel into a canvas bag. 'Right, then, what's with this hen?'

Garry poked me in the back. 'We want to race her,' I gulped.

'Race her?' Alf said in a derisory voice. 'Don't be barmy. She's a crock. You can't go flying a damaged bird. She won't last the length of a football pitch, not on a gammy wing at any rate.'

'But she flies really well, now. Honestly she does.' I gestured to Garry for a bit of support.

'She's dead fast,' he said.

'Really fast,' I added.

'Aye, on a short toss, maybe,' said Alf. 'You let her off in a proper race and she'll be stopping at every chimney-pot she sees. Race her? I've never heard owt so daft.' With an air of finality he zipped up his bag and hoiked it manfully into the lounge. There was a clack of wooden bowls with every step he took. It sounded like his knees were knocking together.

'Please, Mr Duckins,' I pleaded with him, tripping at his heels like a faithful dog. 'Mr Weaver at the basket works, he said we should do it.'

Alf dropped his bag on the end of the sofa and paused at the mirror to comb his hair. 'George Weaver wants his brains examined,' he sniffed.

Garry snorted and stuffed his hands in his pockets. He tilted his head towards St Wilfred's Road, but I wasn't ready to give up yet. 'He said we could put her in a novice event. He said there might be one this Saturday morning. He said you'd help us with . . .y'know, everything.'

'Oh, did he,' Alf said, smoothing his hair. He pulled a handkerchief out of his trouser pocket and blew his nose with a terrifying snort. He looked at me and I nodded like mad.

'He said racing birds were born to race and that pigeon racing was . . . a rewarding hobby for a boy to get into. Please, Mr Duckins. *You* must have started when you were quite young.'

'We're twelve,' said Garry.

Alf sighed and shook his head. 'No. You can't race her. You can't race that bird.'

'Why not?' Garry snapped.

'Because,' Alf huffed. We waited for him to

tell us what. He muttered something rude under his breath. 'You haven't got ... the proper equipment,' he spluttered, throwing up a hand and waving us away.

'Equipment?' Garry sneered. 'She doesn't need equipment. She doesn't have to wear a crash helmet, does she?'

'I mean a clock,' Alf grizzled. 'You haven't got a clock – a proper *racing* clock,' he added, anticipating another of Garry's daft replies. Garry wasn't about to let him down.

'I've got a diver's watch with seconds hands on it.'

'That's not a *proper* clock,' Alf tutted. He sighed at Garry's ignorance and walked to the window, peering through the curtains for the taxi he'd ordered.

'This is stupid,' Garry moaned, not caring if Alf could hear him or not. 'Come on. Let's go and do a good sport – like football.'

Shut up-pp, I mouthed and turned to face Mr Duckins again. 'Can't we borrow a clock, Mr Duckins?'

'You'd have to be in a club,' Alf muttered.

'I know!' I spoke up, getting suddenly excited. I'd almost forgotten about joining a club.

'He's got six quid,' Garry spat out curtly.

'How much does it cost to be in a club?'

I dug about in my pocket and brought out the change I'd kept from Weaver's. I held it out for Mr Duckins to see. 'I can get some more at the weekend,' I said.

'Put it away,' Mr Duckins sighed.

'But—'

'Put it away,' he said more firmly, and looked as if he was going to add something when suddenly his eyes glazed over slightly and he paused as if he was lost in time. He blinked and staggered forward in small shuffled steps, groping like a blind man for the arm of the sofa. I moved forward to support him as he tried to sit down. He gripped my arm with the strength of a monkey. His other hand felt for the centre of his chest.

'All right,' he said. 'I'm all right now.' I stepped back a pace and glanced at Garry. Garry was looking pale and concerned.

'Now, listen,' Alf said through a wheezy breath. 'I can see why you're keen to get into the game, and you're right, it is a grand sport to follow. But there are certain things you don't understand.'

'Like what?' said Garry, politely for once.

'Like the rules,' Alf said, putting back his

shoulders to catch a deep breath. He looked like he'd just had his lungs pumped up. 'Even if that bird can perform like she used to, it's not a simple matter for you to race her.'

'Are we really too young?' I said disappointed.

'No,' said Alf. 'It's nowt to do with that.'

'What then?' I said.

Alf clicked his tongue. His mouth set into a rigid line. 'It's her ring,' he said. 'Her registration. When it comes to marking her up . . .' He gave me a very deliberate stare then turned his chiselled features away.

I blinked in thought, my senses swirling. I guessed Alf was trying to tell me something, more than he really wanted to say – but I just couldn't grasp what it was. I picked my fingers and hesitantly asked, 'Can you get her registered for me, Mr Duckins?'

Before Alf could answer, two things happened: outside, a car horn beeped; inside, Alf gasped and clutched at his chest.

'What's the matter?' said Garry, looking alarmed.

I stepped quickly forward and knelt by Alf's side. 'Mr Duckins? Are you all right? Mr Duckins? Do you want us to ring an ambulance for you?'

'Chest . . .' he spluttered, gasping for breath. 'Pills . . .' He started to beat his pockets.

'Where are they?' I asked, feeling in his pockets. 'Where are your pills?'

Alf raised a shaky finger. He pointed at the table near the patio doors.

'Get them, quick!' I shouted at Garry. Garry ran to the table and was back in a blink.

'These?' he said urgently, holding up a bottle.

Mr Duckins grabbed it and unscrewed the top. He ladled two tablets into his palm, picked them up and placed them under his tongue. Outside, the car horn beeped again.

'Taxi . . .' Alf mumbled. 'Tell him to wait.'

I nodded at Garry. Garry scrambled out the door.

'Please, Mr Duckins, get well,' I said.

Alf gripped my arm and sank back on the sofa. 'Be all right in a minute,' he nodded.

'I'm sorry,' I said, biting my lip. 'I didn't mean to get you upset or anything.'

Alf smiled weakly and shook his head. 'Not your fault. You're a good lad,' he said. His gaze rolled freely across the room.

'What?' I said. 'What do you want?'

'Notepad,' he croaked. 'Probably by the phone.'

I dashed to the phone, found the pad and hurried back.

'Telephone number,' Alf instructed.

'Whose?' I said.

'Yours, you banana.' His breaths were coming easier now and the gruffness was already back in his voice. I scribbled my number down on the pad.

'No promises,' said Alf, 'but I'll see about your bird. I'll ring the club secretary. See what might be done.'

'Aw, thanks, Mr Duckins.' I was almost in tears.

'No promises,' he said. But I knew he was going to try really hard.

At that point Garry burst in through the door. 'I've told him to wait,' he panted loudly. 'He wants to know if you're going to die?'

I slapped a hand across my face.

Alf stood up gingerly and picked up his bag. 'No, I'm just going to play bowls,' he said.

CHAPTER SIXTEEN

'AW, MU-UM! I'M NOT GOING! NO! NO! NO! I'M NOT GOING! I'M NOT! NOT THIS WEEKEND! NO!'

Mum folded her arms and looked at me sternly. 'Darryl, I am going to count to ten. By the time I've reached eight you are going to have stopped this silly tantrum and you and I are going to have a little *chat*.'

'I'M NOT GOING!' I shouted, 'I DON'T *WANT* TO CHAT!'

'One . . .' Mum started.

'Two!' said Natalie.

'Natalie, be quiet,' Mum said brusquely.

'I want to count as well,' said Natalie.

'I'm not GOING,' I snapped.

'Three . . .' counted Mum.

'I *wonder* why Darryl doesn't want to go to Grandma's?'

'Oh, SHUT-UP!' I shouted.

'Four . . .' said Mum.

Just then Dad walked into the lounge. 'What on earth's going on?' he demanded. 'I can hear him through the sound of my razor.'

'Darryl has got a little problem,' said Mum.

'No I haven't,' I snapped.

'Watch your tongue,' Dad warned. 'What problem?'

'It's not a problem for ME!' I hit back.

Dad pointed a finger. 'One more line like that, my lad, and you'll have *two* problems. One of them with me.'

I flopped down in a chair and turned my back on them all.

'He's entered Cherokee into a race,' Mum said.

'I want to be in a race!' said Natalie.

'And?' said Dad.

Mum tidied some newspapers off the coffee table. 'The race is this weekend, when we're supposed to be going to my mother's.'

'I'm not *going*,' I muttered through a tear-stained cushion.

'See?' said Mum.

I heard Dad sigh. 'Don't you think you should have shared this information with us, Darryl? EXCUSE ME, YOUNG MAN, I'M SPEAKING TO YOU!'

'I didn't know till yesterday,' I argued back. 'Mr Duckins rang up and said if I take Cherokee to his house on Friday he'll put her in a race on Saturday morning and give me a proper timing clock and show me what I have to do and that if she comes home it'll only take her two hours and I have to BE *HERE* TO GET HER IN. I HATE YOU. I DON'T WANT TO GO TO GRANDMA'S. I WANT TO RACE MY RACING PIGEON!'

Dad sighed again and plonked his hands on his hips.

'Quite the little professional, isn't he?' said Mum.

'I want to go to Grandma's,' said Natalie.

'We are *all* going to Grandma's,' Dad said firmly.

'NO!' I cried and beat the cushion.

'You can moan as much as you like,' Dad said.

'You do not make arrangements like this without consulting me or your mother first.'

'I hate you,' I mumbled.

'Too bad,' said Dad. 'You'll just have to ask Garry to see Cherokee home.'

I sat up smartly, betrayal written all over my face. 'She's MY BIRD!'

Dad looked at me with great disappointment. 'I thought,' he said slowly, 'that Garry was your friend? If you value his friendship you'll be only too pleased to let him help.'

'He doesn't know what to do!' I argued.

'Then teach him,' Dad snapped. 'Now no more moaning.'

'Oh, fff!' I sniffed and hugged the cushion.

'Don't you dare say a swear word,' Mum warned darkly.

'I know a swear word,' Natalie piped up. 'SAUSAGES!' she cried. 'Sausages! Sausages!'

'Shut up,' I said.

'Sausages,' she said and stuck out her tongue.

'That'll do,' said Mum. She turned to me. 'How's Cherokee getting to this race, anyway? How far is she flying?'

'A hundred miles,' I answered grumpily.

'Where from?' asked Dad. 'North or south?'

'Sausages!' said Natalie.

'Hush,' said Mum.

'Thirsk,' I muttered. 'I think it's north.'

'Thirsk?' Mum said. She raised an eyebrow at Dad. Dad thought a moment, stroking his chin. 'What time on Saturday are the birds released?'

'Dunno,' I shrugged.

'Find out,' said Dad, and turned to leave the room. At the door he stopped and spoke over his shoulder. 'Your gran lives seventeen miles from Thirsk . . .'

CHAPTER SEVENTEEN

'Ooh, yes,' cooed Grandma, not unlike a pigeon, 'your Grandad Thornton was very fond of birds.'

'The feathered variety, I hope,' Mum muttered.

'Mu-um,' I groaned.

Gran laughed it off. 'It's all right,' she said as the car responded with a throaty *vroom* and we shot past a truck carrying farm machinery. 'I was always your grandad's favourite hen.'

I smiled and she gave me a misty-eyed look. I could believe my gran would be anybody's favourite. She was warm and kind – and funny, too. I wondered if she missed my grandad much. I'd never really known my Grandad Thornton. He'd died when I was four years old. It made me feel strangely warm inside to know he had been a pigeon man once. I was keeping up the family tradition and I felt that Gran was proud of me. I was glad she was here to see Cherokee fly. I only wished Grandad could be with us as well.

'Were they just racing pigeons, Mum?' Dad glanced at Gran in the rear-view mirror. He flicked the indicator switch on the steering column. A bright green arrow ticked and flashed. The car veered smoothly up a slip road to the left. A sign saying 'Thirsk' and another with a racehorse painted on it whizzed by. My heart began to pulse with anticipation. The race-track at Thirsk was where Cherokee and the other birds would be released.

'Mostly,' Gran answered. 'It's so long ago, now. He kept racers – and fancy birds as well, if I remember. Tumblers, I think. Hmm, tumblers.'

'What's a tumbler?' asked Mum, just pipping me to it.

'I've got a tumbler!' Natalie interjected, slapping her picture book down on her knees. 'It's got an elephant and a monkey and a giraffe on, Grandma.'

'Lovely,' Gran said. 'I shall have to have some jungle juice out of that.'

'All right,' Natalie chirped and went back to her reading.

'Thank you,' Mum muttered. 'Normal service will now be resumed.'

Gran chuckled softly. 'A tumbler is a bird that does somersaults in the air.'

'Somersaults?' I said.

'Somersaults?' Mum repeated. 'What on earth for?'

'For show,' Dad reasoned. 'I've seen them on the telly. Has Mr Duckins got any show birds, Darryl?'

'Don't think so,' I muttered, staring through the window at the rolling fields. In the distance I could see a number of people cantering horses. Any minute now we were going to be there.

'Is Mr Duckins the chap who's helping you out?'

I turned to Gran and nodded. 'He's going to see if I can join his club. I had to take Cherokee to him on Friday night so she could be registered and brought up here on a pigeon transporter. He's let me borrow a special timing clock, Gran.'

'Oh, yes,' said Gran. 'I remember those. Strange contraptions. They look a bit like podgy barometers. You have a little thimble that you put inside, don't you? But . . . shouldn't you be at the other end for that part, Darryl?'

I gave her a sort of cheesy grin. In two hours' time Garry would be at 'the other end', ready and waiting in our garden at home, watching the skies for Cherokee's arrival. I only hoped he'd do everything right. On Friday night when we'd taken Cherokee to St Wilfred's Road, Mr Duckins had had to explain to him twice what needed doing with the timing clock:

'When she comes in, get hold of her – sharpish. She'll have a special rubber ring on this foot here.' He pointed to her unringed leg. 'All you have to do is pull it off gently – gently, mind – and pop it into this.' He held up a little thimble-like container. 'The details of the race are stamped on that ring, so don't go playing conkers with it or dropping it down the nearest drain. When the ring's in the thimble, put the - thimble in the clock.' He pointed to a slot in the large, round clock. 'The clock'll record your finishing time.'

'What then?' asked Garry.

'That's it, you're done. Bring the clock to me and I'll take it to the stewards.'

'When do we get the money?' said Garry, looking sheepishly at me as soon as he'd said it.

Alf gave him a tortuous look. 'I'll let you know if you win . . .' he growled.

'Here we are,' said Dad. My mind snapped instantly back to the present. The car had just turned off the main road and was travelling along a winding approach to the racecourse buildings. In the distance, the grandstand stood out against the sky, a bit like one quarter of an unfinished football ground. Beyond it I could pick out the actual rails of the course itself. Then suddenly, to my right, I saw something else.

'There it is!' I shouted, straining at my seat-belt. 'Over there, Dad! Drive over there!'

'Calm down,' Mum tutted.

'I see it,' said Gran.

'I want to see it!' Natalie cried, not even knowing what 'it' was.

We could all see it now – a huge transporter, parked on an area of open land about five hundred metres from the racecourse stables. It was stacked with rows of wicker baskets. Panniers, Mr Duckins called them. Inside one of those panniers was Cherokee Wonder.

'Hold tight,' said Dad as we turned off the road and bumped along the uneven, dew-laden grass.

'What time is it?' I barked.

'Ten to eight,' Dad answered.

I bit my lip. Ten minutes. In ten minutes' time, Cherokee Wonder would be in the air, racing. I dipped into my jacket for the scrap of paper with her ring number on it. I wanted to see her before they set her free. To show her I was there, supporting her. I wanted to wave bye-bye as well – just in case . . . 'No,' I said breathily, fogging up the window. 'You will come back. I *know* you will.'

The car wheeled round and stopped nose to nose with the giant transporter. 'Right . . .' Mum started in her 'giving orders' voice. But I was already out and running to the panniers. There was no time for lectures or 'Here's what we're going to do's. Mr Duckins had said the birds would be 'up' at eight o'clock sharp. If I wanted to see Cherokee, I didn't have much time.

I ran alongside the wall of baskets, looking frantically for a small pied hen with a slightly bumpy wing. The air rumbled with the sound of impatient pigeons. They wooed and cooed and shed feathers through the wicker. They strutted and turned and strutted again, beaks knocking at the catches that would soon set them free, eyes tilting at the pale blue sky.

'Hello, what have we here?' said a voice.

An untidy-looking man with his shirt only half-tucked into his trousers limped up beside me. He was smoking a cigarette that drooped off his lip like a wet blade of grass. A badge saying 'North of England Homing Union – Steward' was pinned to his shirt.

'Good Lord,' said Dad, before I could answer. He came strolling up, having a look at the baskets. 'What a commotion. Is it always like this?'

'You a flying man?' the steward asked Dad.

'Uh-uh,' Dad went. The steward's gaze fell on me. My face turned redder than tomato sauce.

'First time?' coughed the steward.

I nodded fiercely. 'Do you know where –' I read out Cherokee's ring number '– is?'

The steward took the piece of paper. 'Which club?' he asked.

'Barrowmoor.'

He nodded and beckoned me towards the baskets. By now, a second steward had appeared. A roly-poly sort of man with a tuft of hair above each of his ears that flapped like two grey wings in the breeze.

'Barrowmoor, Bert?' the first steward shouted.

Bert, the roly-poly man, climbed the transporter. 'This lot,' he shouted, indicating a line of baskets about four rows up. 'What is it you want?'

'A pied hen!' I shouted.

The roly-poly man inspected the baskets. 'This one,' he said – and suddenly I saw her. She came to the front and looked down at me with her brilliant copper eye. In that moment everything we'd done together flooded through my mind: the park; Alf washing her; her flight in the shed; me taking her to school and now . . . now this. My eyes welled with tears.

'Fly,' I whispered. 'Fly, Cherokee. Fly.' I bent my fingers in a single wave then let them roll into a tightly-clenched fist.

'Time to free them, lad,' the steward said.

Dad came up and put an arm around my shoulder. 'Come on,' he said, in a comforting voice, 'let's watch from over here.'

He hugged me all the way back to the car where Mum and Gran and Natalie were waiting. Everyone seemed to be beating their arms or stamping their feet. Natalie had a bonnet and ear muffs on. I hadn't noticed till then how cold it was.

'I wish they'd get on with the race,' Mum chattered, her words hidden behind clouds of breath.

'Thirty seconds to lift off,' said Dad, rubbing his hands as he checked his watch.

'I bet that chap must be feeling it,' said Gran. 'Imagine painting pictures on a morning like this.'

We all looked across the open field. Some way to the side of the pigeon transporter sat a thin-faced man behind a large white easel. He was wearing an anorak and wellington boots. The anorak had plenty of paint splashes on it. He was dabbing at the canvas with confident strokes, constantly angling his head to one side to look at the subject then again at his picture. I wondered if he was the same man who did the paintings in *Spines*. He was an awful long way from home if he was.

'Ready?' a loud voice shouted to us.

Dad stuck up a thumb. We all shuffled round to get a slightly better look, just as the roly-poly steward pulled a cord and the whole bottom row of baskets opened.

'Help!' Mum screamed laying her hands across her ears. The clatter of wings was like a cannon going off. I jumped so much I almost fell over backwards. Birds exploded into the sky: grey, white, blue, brown, shading the sun in a weaving cloud of interlocking wingbeats. Dust and grass bits whirled off the ground, sucked up like a sandstorm into our faces. The air was ripped apart with noise. First the deafening crash of release, then a slow, whirring, helicopter hum as the birds gained pace and climbed into the sky.

'Wow!' Dad cried. 'That's FANTASTIC!' Natalie yelped and danced with delight. Even Mum managed to smile through the shock and the turbulence. But it was Gran who described it best of all:

'Better than Bonfire Night!' she shouted. 'Wheee!' She waved her gloves in the air.

Bang! The second row of panniers opened. This time I didn't jump so much and watched which way the birds were going. They staggered upwards like a swarm of bees, gradually thinning out into a narrow spiral as they joined the first wave circling in the sky.

'Isn't this cheating?' Mum shouted out, still with her hands laid flat to her ears.

'Those birds have got a head start on ours!'

The thin steward heard her and walked across. 'If you let them all go at once,' he said, 'there'd be accidents in the lower tiers – birds hitting the ground, wings bashing together—' *Bang!* The third tier of birds went up, layer upon layer, stirring up the clouds. The steward waited for the noise to subside. '—They'll circle up there for several minutes, get their bearings, then all go off together. That's when the race starts proper.'

'Get ready!' Dad shouted. 'She's towards the far end!' He gripped my shoulder and pointed at the baskets. It was time for Cherokee's row to be released.

'Fly!' I screamed as the clatter came again and they all swept out. 'Fly, Cherokee! Cherokee, fly!'

'Come on–nn!' Mum whooped, flailing her arms.

'Come back safely!' I heard Dad yell through the cup of his hands.

'Can you see her?' Gran asked. 'Can anybody see her?' I shook my head. I'd tried to focus on her basket alone but she was lost as soon as the wave broke out. But I was sure she was up there racing for her life, winging her way back home to Garry – and who knows, winning us a prize as well.

But I was wrong.

As the fifth and final row went up, one bird fluttered back to earth. There was silence as everybody followed its descent. It landed with a slightly ungracious bounce, stood for a moment, then started to potter around the field.

'Oh no,' said Dad, 'you don't think . . . ?'

But I did think. I was already running across the grass.

'Is that yours?' I heard a steward ask Dad. 'It's pied, I think. Didn't you have a pied?'

It *was* a pied bird. And I *knew* it was Cherokee, well before I was close enough to see for sure. I closed in urgently, desperate to catch her, terrified she might flutter off after all, only to come down two miles away, lost and confused, gone for ever. I called her name. The sound made her jump and she did flutter off, but only as far as the man with the easel. He blinked in surprise and put down his brush. Then he stood up calmly and walked right to her. With one confident swoop he scooped her up off the ground.

I was at his side in a matter of seconds.

'She yours?' he said, examining her ring.

'Yes,' I said with a lump in my throat. 'She can

fly really well. She's hurt her wing, that's all.' I felt angry having to give an excuse. I just didn't want anyone laughing at her. But the artist wasn't laughing at her. He had a thoughtful look in his dark blue eyes. He turned it on me as he ran his fingers over her wing, feeling the swelling at the shoulder carefully. 'Hmm,' he murmured, 'nasty break. If you want my advice you won't go trying this much more.' He nodded once at the pigeon transporter. Then he held Cherokee out and I took her from him.

'Thanks,' I said in a wimpy voice.

The stranger smiled, barely moving his lips. 'You've done well with her,' he said. 'Most birds don't survive a break like that.'

I stroked her neck and gave a modest shrug.

He smiled again. 'You're Alf's boy, aren't you?'

Suddenly, my whole world seemed to freeze. My brain, already muzzy with disappointment, heaped confusion in on top. 'How? How did you know that?' I stuttered.

The stranger flipped a cigarette out of a packet and knocked both ends of it against the box. 'I'm from Barrowmoor,' he said. 'The name's Lenny Spigott. I was wondering when I might bump into you.'

CHAPTER EIGHTEEN

For a moment, it was all I could do to stop from falling over. My legs felt thinner than two blades of grass. There was a buzzing in my ears that was making me dizzy. Lenny Spigott calmly lit up his cigarette and frowned.

'I . . . I . . . I didn't steal her,' I blabbered, stumbling backwards, holding Cherokee tight to my chest. 'Mr Duckins said . . . you didn't want her. He said you were going to wring her neck. He said if I took her it would be all right. I only—'

'Calm down,' Lenny cut in, blowing a column of smoke. 'Nobody's accusing you of stealing her. If I was I'd hardly give her back to you, would I? You can keep the bird. I've a loft full at home.'

'I – what?'

'You keep her, lad. You deserve to have her. I couldn't have attended to her in that state, anyway. I mean it. She's yours. You want her, don't you?'

I nodded, keeping my face well down. I was shaking with fear and couldn't seem to get my thoughts in focus. Was it true? Did Lenny *really* mean it? Was he genuinely giving Cherokee to me? Or was it all just a horrible joke? A Warren-type torture? I needed to know.

'How did you . . . ? I mean . . . ? Who told you . . . ? WHO TOLD YOU I'D KEPT HER?' I spat out harshly.

'Steady on,' frowned Lenny, pulling back. 'What's eating you now? Duckins told me.'

'Alf?' I queried.

'Aye,' he grizzled. 'Wheezy Alf. Who else knew you'd got the bird?'

Your son, I thought. Warren knew. My mind went through a frantic hoop-la. But if it really wasn't Warren who'd told his dad . . . and Lenny Spigott didn't mind anyway, then . . . I started to pant with nervous excitement. *Please*, I was

152

thinking. *Don't let it be a trick. Please. Not now. Please let her be mine.*

'Honestly?' I blurted, crossing my fingers. 'Was it honestly Alf who told you I'd got her?'

Lenny took a puzzled drag on his cigarette. 'Aye, shall I write it on the grass or what? Alf rang me, middle of last week. He told me you'd nursed the hen back to health and were knocking his door down to get her in a race. I thought it was a barmy idea, but he asked if I'd sort it as a favour to him. He told me you were a good lad, helped him over one of his attacks. He's not a well man, you know, is Alf.'

I nodded, but I was still confused. 'You mean . . . ? You *knew* I was going to race her?'

'I've just said so, haven't I?'

'I know. But . . . why? Why did he have to ask you about it?'

Lenny shrugged as if the answer was obvious. 'Officially, the hen still belongs to me. You can't race a bird unless she's registered in your name. There was no time to get the paperwork changed. So I raced her for you. It was the easiest way. I'm a bit surprised to find you here, though. Shouldn't you be at the other end, waiting?'

But I didn't quite hear the last remark. My

mind was drifting back to the night of Alf's bowls match. So *that's* why he'd tried to put me off. The registration. The proper procedures. If a steward had looked at Cherokee's ring they would know she still belonged to Lenny. Slowly, the murk was beginning to clear.

'You mean . . . if she'd won, you'd have got the money?'

Lenny roared with laughter and shook his head. 'She was never going to win the race,' he said. He clocked the hurt in my eyes and drew a bit closer, rubbing a knuckle down Cherokee's neck. 'Listen, lad. I'll be straight with you. I agreed to this business because Alf's a good friend . . . but we both knew she might pull a stunt like this. These birds have got more cokum than most folks give them credit for. She knew what she was here for and she wasn't prepared to go through with the effort. I didn't think she'd pack in quite so early, though; I imagined she'd end up on some Town Hall square, scrapping for chip ends and bits of bread.'

'You mean—?'

'I mean, I didn't expect you'd see her again.' He quickly raised a hand. 'And before you start giving me the evil eye, we did it in the best interests of you *and* the bird.' He blew a final pother of smoke into the sky and flicked the cigarette butt on to the grass. 'You can't keep a solitary pigeon, son. These birds like to flock; they need the company of others. Sooner or later she'd have left your roost and flapped off in search of a cock to mate with. That's their way. Better you lost her in the middle of a race than be heartbroken, searching the rooftops of Barrowmoor. Do you see what I'm saying?'

I nodded sadly and stroked her back.

'So,' said Lenny, 'there it is. If you want to do what's right for her, take her to the country and let her go. Unless . . .'

I looked up.

'Unless you intend to start a loft, of course.'

'Alf said I could join his club,' I muttered.

'Fair enough,' Lenny smiled. 'That's your answer. If you need some advice about starting up, come and see me sometime. I'll show you what's needed.'

My mouth fell open in shock. Me? Go to Warren Spigott's house?

'I'm serious,' said Lenny. 'I'll always help anyone who wants to keep birds. Pigeons and painting—they're my life.'

I swallowed hard and gave him a grateful nod. Then I remembered something Alf had

155

once said and began to feel all sheepish again. 'Mr Spigott?'

'Hmm?'

'Mr Duckins said you don't like kids very much. So . . . ?'

Lenny clamped his teeth and grimaced slightly. He glanced away across the open fields. 'Aye, well. There are kids and there are kids. If you'd seen the animal I feed at home you might understand the reason why.' He patted me on the shoulder. 'Your dad's here, I think.'

'All right, Darryl?' Dad asked, striding up. 'Your mum and Natalie are getting a bit chilly. We ought to be heading back to Gran's house soon. Is Cherokee OK?'

I blushed and went all soppy a moment. 'That's what I call her,' I explained to Lenny.

He looked at Dad and smiled. 'Len Spigott,' he said, thrusting out a hand for Dad to shake. 'I've just been giving your boy some advice.'

'Mr Spigott comes from Barrowmoor, Dad. He used to own Cherokee before we did.'

'Really?' Dad raised an eyebrow. 'That's a bit of an odd coincidence.'

'Long story,' said Lenny, winking at me.

'And are you taking . . . ?' Dad gestured at Cherokee.

'Oh no,' said Lenny. 'She belongs to Darryl, now. It's all official – well, it would be if we did it properly. I don't suppose you need it in writing, do you?'

I forced a strained smile onto my lips. I knew Lenny had said what he had in jest, but for me the words had a chilling significance. At the risk of breaking his trust, I said, 'Please, Mr Spigott. Would it be all right? To have it in writing, I mean?'

'Tch,' Dad tutted. 'We're grooming him to be a solicitor, you know.'

Lenny grunted with laughter and felt his pockets. We all felt our pockets. No-one had a pen.

'Tell you what,' Lenny chuckled. 'I'll paint it for you. In nice big letters. Very official. I take it paint'll be all right? You don't want it in blood, I hope?'

No, I was thinking. *I didn't want blood.*

I wanted revenge.

And genuine proof that Cherokee was mine.

CHAPTER NINETEEN

Since the night we'd escaped through the spinney for the bus, I'd managed to avoid Warren Spigott and his gang. I hadn't heard his whistle all the next day, or the next. And I was half-praying, half-hoping that he'd finished school or something and wouldn't bully me or make me be his slave again. Then one afternoon during football practice I heard Connor Dorley moaning like mad about the fourth years going on a Geography trip and how we never got to do things like that. And I knew it was only a matter of time before Warren and his whistle and his threats came back.

But when he did, I was going to be ready for him.

Back at school, on Monday, after our visit to Gran's, I heard his whistle twice at dinner.

'He's gonna be so-oooo mad,' said Garry as we hid in the mats cupboard in the junior gym. 'He's gonna mash you into . . . mashed potato.'

I felt really comforted by *that*, of course. 'After school,' I trembled. 'We'll go to him then.'

'We?' Garry queried, turning pale.

'I need a witness,' I said. 'Four o'clock. OK?'

'OK,' he whimpered with a bit of a gulp. 'I hope you know what you're doing, though . . .'

I did. I had a plan. But as usual, it didn't quite run to schedule . . .

'ON YOUR WAY OUT,' Mr Tompkins bellowed over the sound of the final bell, 'DON'T FORGET TO LEAVE LAST WEEK'S HOME-WORK ON MY DESK!'

'Oh no!' I gasped. I clamped my hands across my face and lowered my head with a *thunk!* on the desk. Homework. I'd forgotten to do my

English homework! Five hundred words about . . . what was it again?

'Something the matter, Darryl?'

Mr Tompkins had spotted my reaction straight away. And from the look on his face he'd guessed the reason for it.

'What you gonna do?' Garry hissed at me urgently, taking his workbook out of his bag. 'He'll make you stay behind for sure.'

'Darryl?' Mr Tompkins enquired sternly, casting his eyes towards the growing pile of workbooks on his desk.

'I'll see you at your place,' Garry whispered nervously.

'No!' I grabbed his arm and tugged. 'Wait for me outside.'

Garry screwed his face into a pained expression. 'You're mad,' he muttered.

But I knew he'd wait.

'Well, Darryl?' Mr Tompkins said again as Garry handed in his homework and backed out of the room. I hadn't even bothered to get up from my desk.

'Sorry, sir. I forgot.'

'Forgot.'

'Yes, sir.'

'I see. Despite our little chat this time last

week you couldn't even *remember* your home-work – let alone do it?'

I squirmed and hung my head in shame.

'Look at me,' Mr Tompkins snapped. I brought my head up. 'Do you have an excuse?' I shook my head. Mr Tompkins scowled. 'Well, would you like to tell me what you *have* been doing all this week?'

I shrugged awkwardly, trying to remember. All I could think of was the visit to Gran's.

'Pigeons.' Mr Tompkins sighed in defeat. 'Well, Darryl, you leave me no choice.' He paused to let my discomfort sink in. *Please*, I was thinking, *please don't say you'll tell my mum.* He didn't. He shook his head in despair. Then he stood up and rolled the blackboard round. The list of words was still written on it. 'Right,' he said. 'If you can't find the time to do your homework, I will simply have to find it for you. There is your list. Take out your workbook and get on with it – now. Five hundred words. That's about two sides. And I don't want to hear a SOUND until you've finished.' He snatched Garry's workbook off the top of the pile, shook it meaningfully, and was just about to sit down and mark it when . . .

Phreeep!

Warren's whistle sounded. I jumped so hard my knees hit the desk.

'Right,' snapped Mr Tompkins, whacking Garry's workbook down on his desk. He peered angrily through the window then turned on his heels and in four long strides was at the classroom door. 'I am going to find that foolish boy and bring him *and* his whistle in here!'

'What?' I squeaked.

'Get on with your essay!'

'Yes, sir,' I said, shaking like a leaf. I unzipped my pencil case and took out a pen.

I wrote like I only had minutes to live, so fast my pen was almost ripping up the paper. I thought if I could fill two sides of my workbook before Mr Tompkins returned with Warren, I could leave the essay safely on his desk and slip out before either of them saw me. I scrawled the word COURAGE on the top of a page and underlined it twice in bright red ink. I didn't even bother to check the other words. I already knew a good example of courage. I wanted to write how Cherokee Wonder had battled against the pain of a broken wing and conquered her injuries to fly again. But as I started to write, things boiled up inside me. All the hurt and frustration of the last few weeks, the worry, the stealing, the fears about losing my wonder bird. It all frothed up and spilled out on to the paper. *Sometimes*, I wrote, *people think it is good and clever to try and take away something precious from you. They do it because it makes them look big, in front of their friends. But they are not big, really. They are not brave, either. They are mean and spiteful and nasty and unimportant. They do not understand what courage really is. Courage is flying with a broken wing, even when you know you will fall to the ground. Courage is standing up to people, even when you know they can knock you down . . .*

Wham!

The classroom door nearly rocked off its hinges. Mr Tompkins swept in chuntering to himself. 'Been all the way round the flaming school and he's still managed to give me the blasted slip.' He glanced at me as if I was to blame. 'Get on with your work,' he commanded and sat down.

'But I've finished, sir,' I said. I'd done . . . two and a *half* sides. I couldn't believe it. It wasn't even my biggest writing.

'What?' Mr Tompkins checked his watch. 'Up here, let me see it,' he said suspiciously.

I walked to the front and handed it over. He waved blindly at a desk and started to read. I tutted impatiently and flopped into a chair.

About three minutes later he sat back drumming his fingers on the desk. He gave me his horrible searchlight look, the one that digs about in all your murkiest corners. 'This essay,' he purred, 'it's very good.'

I blushed with surprise. I'd only scrambled it down.

'Are you aware what it is you've been writing about?'

'Courage, sir,' I said, confused.

He shook his head. 'You use the word a lot but this is really a piece about cowardice, Darryl. And it's not really about Cherokee Wonder, is it?'

I shrugged, but my shoulders felt very tight.

'Do you want to tell me who it *is* about?'

There was a pause. All the silence in the world seemed to be ganging up at once, until suddenly it was shattered . . . by a blast from *that* whistle.

'Hhh!' I froze in an open-mouthed position. I was shaking so hard my knuckles were rapping Morse code on the desk. 'C-can I go now, sir?'

Mr Tompkins observed me over steepled fingers. Then he turned his head slowly and glanced through the window. 'Hmm,' he said thoughtfully. 'Go on. Scarper.'

He still hadn't moved when I whizzed through the door.

It didn't take me long to find Warren Spigott. As I scooted down the path between the Arts and Science blocks, Garry stepped out of the shadows of the bike sheds. We headed for the hedges that ran behind the playing fields. Warren and Ginger were waiting for us.

'About time,' snarled Warren, flicking away a fag. He whipped his hair off his forehead with an angry swipe. 'Where've you been, you miserable tyke?' He blew his whistle really loud and dug a finger at the patch of ground in front of him. He looked as if lightning would flash from his arms. He was mad enough to burn, that was for sure.

But I took my time. I walked up slowly, never once taking my eyes off his face.

'Come on-nn,' he shouted. 'Aren't you forgetting something? What is it you're supposed to say to me, slave?'

I took a nervous gulp and stopped short of where he wanted me. I could feel Garry's breath on the back of my neck. 'I'm not going to be your slave any more.'

Warren's dark eyes narrowed. I could see now how much he resembled his father. But there wasn't an ounce of caring in his face — only hatred and vague surprise. 'You what?' he growled. '*What* did you say?'

Suddenly, the pressure got to Garry and he cracked. 'Your dad knows we've got his pigeon! And he doesn't care, either! And we can *prove* it!'

'Who rattled your cage?' Ginger said stepping forward. He lashed out and whacked Garry hard across the head.

'Agh! That hurt!' Garry sank down, blubbing, clutching his ear. Ginger spat out some gum and sneered in triumph.

'You leave him!' I screamed, flapping wildly at Ginger. 'It's true! She belongs to me properly now! I saw Warren's dad at a pigeon race and he said I could have her — have her for keeps!'

'You . . .' Ginger started, capturing my arms. He danced me round and flung me at Warren.

'Liar,' Warren sniffed and slapped me on the head. He bundled me back to Ginger again. He kicked me in the knee and sent me sprawling on the grass.

'Look at them,' Warren sneered from above. 'Pathetic little slaves. You're gonna pay double for this, you twerps.'

'No we're not,' I said and scrambled angrily to my feet. I dived into my jacket and they both reeled back as if I might have a gun. But I had something much more powerful than that: a signed statement from Warren's father. 'There!' I yelled, and showed it to them:

I, Leonard Spigott, of Station Road

Barrowmoor

give this pigeon GB96Z54978

to Darryl Otterwell

26th May 1998

This time, Warren looked visibly shaken. His eyes swept scathingly over the document. His thin lips mouthed its contents, twice.

'Gimme that!' He snatched the paper off me.

'No!' I squealed, jumping to retrieve it. That was the only evidence I'd got. Warren examined the writing closely, holding me at bay with one powerful hand.

'We've got a photograph of it,' Garry lied from the ground. 'So we don't even care if you rip it up.'

Ginger flashed Warren a worried glance. Warren snorted and handed the paper to him. 'Well,' he said, shoving me away. 'Looks like they've got us in a corner, Ginge. Clever slaves, huh? We didn't count on that. Unless . . .' He snapped his fingers and smirked at his mate. 'Unless . . .' He swivelled on his heel and swaggered towards me. I backed away, frightened. Somehow, I knew he was really going to blow. 'Unless the cocky little slave has seen my dad's paintings in the window of *Spines* and decided to try and forge his signature . . . ?'

'It's real,' I quivered. 'I *did* see your dad. You ask him. He said I could go and see his pigeons if I—'

'Shut it!' Warren yelled. His hand shot forward and gagged my throat. 'You made it up to try and get out of our little *arrangement*. Well I tell you what, slave. It's gonna be twice as bad from now on. You're gonna buy me anything and everything I want. You're gonna be my slave till the end of your days!'

'I don't think so,' said a voice. 'Now put him down.'

The vice-like hand relaxed its grip. I bent double. A dribble of saliva hit my shoes.

'Just a game, sir,' said Ginger.

'He hit me!' Garry bawled.

'Shut up,' growled Warren.

'No,' said Mr Tompkins, striding forward, 'you're the one who's going to shut up, Spigott.' He held out his hand. 'Come on, hand it over.' Warren thought for a moment, then realized what Mr Tompkins wanted. Grudgingly, he put his hand in his pocket.

Mr Tompkins took the whistle and dropped it on the ground, then stamped it into splinters with the heel of his shoe.

'Head's office. NOW!' he roared at them both.

Warren and Ginger melted away.

Garry looked at me with tears in his eyes.

'We did it,' I said, and pulled him to his feet.

CHAPTER TWENTY

Garry's ear came up like a strawberry patch, all red and blotchy and *very* wounded. It looked brilliant. So did the bruise on my knee. We couldn't wait to tell Connor and the rest of our mates how we'd stood up to Warren and lived to show the scars. We knew they were going to be dead impressed – unlike Mum, who definitely *wasn't* impressed.

'How on EARTH did you get that?' she cried, dragging Garry over to the medicine cabinet and fiddling for a bottle of antiseptic.

'Erm . . . I was chasing Darryl and he erm . . .'

'I don't want to know,' Mum said sharply, pressing a dampened cloth to his ear.

'Ow! But you just asked,' he complained.

'Hold still,' she fussed, clucking like a hen. 'Honestly, Garry Taylor, the amount of patching up I do to you. I sometimes wonder if I shouldn't ring your mother and ask for a swap.'

'Mum,' I interrupted, changing the subject, 'will you give us a lift to Mr Duckins' after tea? We've got to return his timing clock.'

'I suppose so,' she muttered, reaching for a plaster.

'Thanks. See you in the garden, Gazza.'

'Ow!' he moaned again.

'Don't be such a baby,' Mum scolded him.

In the garden, I told Cherokee Wonder everything we'd done. I told her she was mine for ever now and that no-one could possibly take her from me.

'You won't be lonely,' I promised her, kissing her head. 'I'll come and see you three times a day. Even when it snows. Honest, I will.' I kissed her again and let her go. Away she fluttered, up to the chimney-pot, and sat there like a cock on a weather vane.

'You *won't* be lonely,' I promised her again.

But I couldn't rid the nagging doubt from my mind.

Mum dropped us off at Alf's as the light was fading. 'I'm popping up the road to *ShopWise*,' she said. 'Twenty minutes. Will that be enough?'

'Yep,' I said and climbed out of the car.

'And don't go tearing off that dressing, Garry Taylor.'

Garry grimaced by way of reply. He tore the dressing off as soon as the car was out of sight.

On the way up the patchwork drive he said, 'Will you tell Alf everything? You know, about Warren?'

'Not Warren,' I said. 'He might tell Lenny.'

'Hmm,' he nodded. 'What about the race?'

'Dunno,' I shrugged, and rang the bell.

After a minute or so the door swung open. But this time, it wasn't Alf on the step. My jaw dropped open. Garry's eyes nearly popped. Standing in the doorway was a sulky-looking girl.

She was tall and slim with a pouty mouth and hair that curled neatly under her chin. She was in a uniform I didn't recognize at first: black socks, black skirt and a red v-necked sweater. She even had a school tie undone at her neck. I guessed she was a third year, perhaps a bit older. She was looking down on us like a senior anyway.

'Who are you?' said Garry, blunt as ever.

'Who are *you*?' she snapped back, noticing his ear and clicking her tongue in huffy disgust.

'We've come to see Mr Duckins,' I explained, noticing the initials SHSG stitched on her sweater. Spenner Hill School for Girls. That was where Mum wanted to send Natalie when she was old enough. Only really clever girls went to Spenner Hill.

The girl swept her hair aside with what Mum would call 'a petulant flick'. She turned and gave me a sour sort of look. She had a piercing glint in her dark brown eyes and a stance as fierce as a Jack Russell terrier. I could feel the back of my neck turning cold. She was almost as frightening as Warren Spigott.

'We've come to bring him this.' I showed her the clock. 'Can we talk to him, please?'

'Who is it, Susan?' a woman's voice butted in.

'Two boys, Mum.'

A head popped into view above Susan's shoulder. 'Oh.'

'They want to see Grandad.'

'Oh dear,' said the woman. 'Have you explained?'

The girl shook her head. 'I'm going to give Gregory his worming pill,' she said. And with a moody sniff, she drifted down the hall.

'Don't mind Susan, she's upset,' said the woman.

'What's the matter?' I asked. 'Is Alf all right?'

I looked at Garry. He was biting his lip.

'He's in hospital,' Susan's mother explained. 'His heart, I'm afraid—'

'Hhh . . .' Garry shot a hand to his mouth. I thought for a moment he was going to be sick.

'No, don't worry,' the woman assured him, 'he's going to be fine. Do you mind if I ask how you know Mr Duckins?'

I told her briefly and gave her the clock. 'Oh,' she nodded. 'That's very nice. He's very keen on anyone with birds. Susan and I are just helping out until he gets home. I say "I", she's the expert, really. Certainly takes after her grandad, there.'

I forced my lips into a cheesy smile, but I was actually feeling strangely jealous of Susan.

'You could come and give her a hand if you like? She seems to be worming them all tonight.'

I gave a little shrug. 'Mum's picking us up in a minute.'

'Another time, then?'

We nodded and smiled. But I could sense

Garry thinking he'd like to keep a safe-ish distance from Susan.

'Excuse me, Mrs Duck—?'

'—ins,' she finished. 'Yes, I am a Duckins.'

'Who's Gregory?'

Mrs Duckins smiled. 'A red chequer,' she replied. 'The oldest bird Mr Duckins has got. Gregory Peck is his all-time favourite.'

'Gregory *Peck*?' Garry snorted.

Mrs Duckins chuckled. 'It's an old joke,' she said.

'You mean, he gave a bird a *name*?' I asked. That wasn't what he'd told us when we'd first met him.

Mrs Duckins leaned forward and crossed her arms. 'He's a sentimental old duffer at heart,' she said, checking herself slightly at the mention of 'heart'. 'Listen,' she continued brightly, 'if you really want to see him, why don't you both go and pay him a visit?'

'In hospital?' shuddered Garry.

'The Royal,' she nodded. 'Ward Eighteen. You could get someone to look at that ear while you're there . . .'

CHAPTER TWENTY-ONE

'Mr Duckins, *please*,' the nurse said irritably, waving a finger from the bottom of the bed. 'What have I told you about laughing like that? You're supposed to be resting. So please, REST. Don't go getting him excited, you boys.'

'Sorry,' we said.

The nurse frowned and walked away. We both aimed a spiky tongue at her back.

'Wouldn't race,' Alf tittered. 'I like that. I've heard some pigeon stories in my time but that one just about takes the crust. It's a wonder she bothered to leave the pannier! You've got yourself a character there, all right.'

I smiled and wrung my hands in embarrassment. 'It was worth a try though, wasn't it?' I said.

Alf coughed loudly and struggled with his pillows. Garry leapt up and adjusted them for him. 'Aye, it was worth a try. I suppose I'd have done it when I was your age. We all do daft things sometimes, lad.'

'Mr Duckins,' I said, after a pause, 'can I ask you something about my loft?'

'Aye, fire away.'

'Mr Spigott said it wasn't good to keep a single hen. He said she might fly off and go looking for a mate. Is that right? Will she, y'know . . . get lonely?'

Alf stuck his tongue in the side of his cheek. 'Maybe,' he sniffed. 'Maybe not. All birds are different. Hens are a mystery at the best of times.'

It wasn't a very satisfying answer – and Alf seemed to know it himself right away. Before Garry or I could speak again he patted his blankets and said, 'Look, tell you what, when I get right again p'r'aps I should come round and see this loft? It'd be easier to tell you what I think about it then.'

'Would you?' I said, sitting up smartly.

'Ace,' said Garry.

'That's brilliant!' I added. 'Thanks, Mr Duckins!'

Alf shook his head and burst out laughing again.

'Mis-ter *Duckins* . . .' sighed a voice down the ward.

It was one Sunday morning about three weeks later that Alf rang up and arranged to visit. I called Garry over and between us we made sure Cherokee was spotless. First we dipped her and dried her like we'd done before, then we cleaned out her box with disinfectant and scraped all the droppings off the floor of the shed. We even scrubbed the window and the path outside.

'Flipping heck,' Dad whistled, coming to inspect. 'Any volunteers to give the car a wash next?'

'No,' we said with combined voices.

'Thought not,' he sighed. 'Come on, he's here . . .'

'One sugar or two?' Mum was asking as Garry and I walked into the kitchen.

'Hello, Mr Duckins.'

'Hello, Mr Duckins.'

'How do,' he grunted. 'One sugar, please.' Mum nodded and put a biscuit on his saucer, too.

'How are you feeling?' I asked politely. He looked an awful lot better than the last time we'd seen him. His cheeks weren't pale and grey for a start, and he didn't seem to be wheezing much. He was wearing what Mum would call his 'Sunday best' – a pair of flannels and a crisp black blazer with a brightly-coloured scarf tied neatly round his neck.

'Not bad,' he boomed. 'Glad to be back on my feet again.'

Just then, Natalie scooted in. She skidded to a stop in front of Alf, looked curiously at his face, then at something on the floor beside him.

'What have you got in that box?' she asked.

'Box?' muttered Garry. We both leaned over the table to see.

Just beside Alf's chair was a cardboard carrier, a bit like the cat-box we'd used once for Cherokee. For one heart-stopping moment I thought Lenny Spigott had changed his mind and Alf had come to take Cherokee away. Then Natalie crouched to investigate further. Almost

179

immediately she stood up and said, 'You've got a bird.'

'Aye,' said Alf. 'You're right. I have.'

'What?' said Mum, exchanging glances with Dad.

'*We've* got a bird,' Natalie told Alf.

'I know,' replied Alf. 'And soon you'll have another.'

Suddenly, the kitchen went deathly quiet and everyone seemed to be looking at me. 'Another?' I said in an uncertain voice.

'If it's all right with your mum and dad,' said Alf.

Dad gaped like a goldfish. Mum looked a bit confused. 'Well . . .' she floundered, and then she was gaping like a fish as well.

'It's like this,' said Alf, dunking his biscuit. 'I did a lot of thinking while I was laid up in bed, and I've come to the conclusion that I'm far too old and a sight too weary to cope with pigeons at my time of life. And what with my ticker playing up – well, it seems sensible to let the birds go.'

'But . . . won't they come back again?' Garry asked dimly.

'I meant, move them on,' Alf said sadly, clamping his hairy hands together. 'I can't complain. I've had a good run. And it won't happen all at once, of course. I'll see the young birds through another winter, then . . .'

'But . . . where will you take them?' I said a bit warily, aware that Mum and Dad were having a whispered discussion over my head.

'The best'll go to Spigott,' Alf replied. 'And the other fanciers can take their pick of the rest. I've brought you this old feller 'cos I thought he might keep your hen a bit of company.'

'Feller?' Mum jerked. 'You mean it's a male?' She folded her arms and looked worriedly at Dad.

'Erm, look, Mr Duckins . . .' Dad began, rubbing his fingertips against his brow.

'If you're worried about . . . y'know,' Alf cut in, pointing at a poster of baby chickens on the kitchen wall, 'he hasn't got a right lot of go left in him. He hasn't paired up for some time now . . .'

'Paired up?' gabbled Mum.

Garry sniggered. I elbowed him hard. Alf just smiled and picked up the box.

'Why don't we go into the garden?' he said.

We trooped, single-file, up the garden path. All sorts of thoughts were spinning through my head. But what was going through Mum and Dad's minds? Some way behind me I could hear them arguing.

'I thought he was just looking at the shed?' Mum hissed.

'Well *I* didn't know.'

'Well we don't want another.'

Alf stopped by the shed and peeped in through the window.

'Do you want to see inside?' I said, catching up.

'In a minute,' Alf winked. He put down the box and bent to open it. A gruff woo-wooing came from inside. 'Now then, now then. Don't act up.' He stood up stiffly with a bird in his hands. 'This is Gregory Peck,' he announced.

'Hhh!' I gasped.

'Mummy!' cried Natalie, pointing at the bird.

'I can see,' said Mum. 'Gregory *Peck*?'

'He's beautiful,' said Dad.

'Wow,' breathed Garry, stroking its back. 'Isn't that the one . . . ?'

I nodded slowly. It *was* the one. The big old bird with brown and white feathers. The one that Garry had protected from Carrots. The one I'd talked to inside Alf's loft.

'But why?' I said. 'I thought he was your favourite?'

'He is,' said Alf. 'He's a grand old thing. Did I ever tell you why I kept him?'

Garry and I both shook our heads. Alf glanced at Mum. She raised her face to the sky.

'Some years ago,' said Alf, 'must be fifteen now, I lost all my birds bar this one to a virus. He was only a young cock then, of course, but like the others he was very sick. Several times I tried to put him out of his misery, but each time I went to . . .' he glanced at Natalie '. . . do the business, he kept showing me something – some fight, I suppose. So I let him alone, like I'd done with some of the others. Others died. This chap lived. Not only that, he went on to win me lots of races. A proper champion in his day, he was. Made me a very proud man indeed. And I swore— '

'Hhh!' went Natalie.

'—promised,' Alf explained, 'that I would care for him through thick and thin and always provide him with a decent home. That's why I want you to keep him, lad.' He turned and handed him over like a prize. The bird struggled a moment, then was still in my hands. 'No other flying man'll take him on. And when the last of mine are gone and he's left on his tod, I don't want him fretting and withering away. He'll be favourite here, in a loft of his own. No other cocks to bustle him about. Your hen'll keep him tidy, you see. So, if you want him, there he is. My gift for everything you've done for me, and for all you've done for that hen.'

I shuddered. I didn't know what to say. A tear was streaming down my face and that awful silence had descended again. I looked at the champion, Gregory Peck, then turned my bleary gaze on Mum. To my amazement, she was wiping a tear away, too. She and Dad went into a huddle. A few seconds later, Dad called me over.

'You promise to look after both of them properly?'

I gave a sniffy nod.

'Promise?'

'Yes.'

Dad touched a hand to the old bird's neck. 'Gregory *Peck*. All right. He's yours.'

CHAPTER TWENTY-TWO

It didn't take Mum long to get back to normal.
'That flippin' Gregory Peck!' she complained.
'Did a big brown . . . *doing* on my clothes line
last night. And why is he cooing at five in the
mornings!?'

'He's happy,' I said. 'He likes it in the shed.'

'Hmph,' Mum grunted. 'Someone ought to
put a clock in there and tell him to wake at a
decent hour.'

'We could put another nesting box in,' I
suggested.

'Don't push your luck,' she growled back.

She cheered up a few days later, though, when I came home waving my school report. 'Hmm,' she murmured. 'Hmm, not bad. I see there's been some improvement in English.' She passed it over for me to read. Mr Tompkins had written:

Needs to find a subject that interests him, but capable of exceptional ability once found.

I had good reports for Maths and Science, too. 'I did promise to try a bit harder,' I said, all meek and innocent, trying to milk all the praise I could get.

'Yes,' Mum said. 'I'm very pleased. Your dad will be, too. Shows what you can do when you really try.'

'Does this mean I get a reward?' I grinned.

She scrunched up a tea-towel and threw it at me. 'You're a lot chirpier lately . . .' she said.

That was because I owned *two* pigeons now – and I wasn't anybody's slave any more. I saw Warren plenty of times at school. But he never came near me, nor did Ginger. And as the summer holidays began to approach, the fear of seeing them melted away. Garry and I never talked about it.

I liked having two pigeons in the shed. By now, it wasn't really a shed any more. Dad had moved his mower to the garage and carted the old pram off to the tip. Greg and Cherokee had the place to themselves – and I had my very own pigeon loft. It wasn't as smart as Mr Duckins', but he said I'd done well with what I'd got. He made a few suggestions about perches and drinkers and gave Cherokee a worming tablet as well.

Gregory Peck was a brilliant bird. And I finally found out why grown-ups repeated his name when they heard it. 'Gregory Peck was a film star,' said Mum. 'He was famous and hand-some – if you like that kind of thing.'

'Was he Pigeon-Man or something, then?' asked Garry.

'I despair of you, Garry Taylor,' Mum sighed. 'No, it's just his name, I suppose.'

We looked at her blankly.

'Peck,' she emphasised. 'Pigeons peck, don't they?'

'So do chickens,' muttered Garry. 'I wouldn't give a chicken a name like Gregory.'

'Oh . . . peck off!' Mum said curtly. I looked at Garry. He was totally shocked!

For the first few days after I'd got him, I had to leave Gregory in the shed all the time.

'To let him make a roost for himself,' Alf advised.

'But when I do let him out, won't he still fly back to your house anyway?'

'Shouldn't think so,' Alf said. 'He's too lazy to flap much further than a roof top. Besides, he knows he's on to a good thing here.'

He did, too. Every day when I came to feed them I sneaked up secretly to the shed window and had a little peek inside. Greg and Cherokee were always together, standing on top of the nesting box or following each other from one perch to another. He seemed to like to dance in front of her as well. Lots of times I saw him puffing out his chest and fanning his tail-feathers and strutting around. He was a real show-off. One night, when I'd let them out for their exercise, I even saw Gregory taking her presents. He was carrying little bits of twigs into the shed and flying up to the nest box with them.

'Are they in love?' Natalie asked me once.

'Don't be dumb,' I said. But I wasn't too sure.

Then, one night, something dreadful happened. I opened the shed door and called them out, but only Cherokee fluttered into the garden.

'Greg?' I said, looking round the shed. I

couldn't see him anywhere. My heart began an anxious thump. 'Greg?' I repeated, and stepped inside.

I found him sitting in the nesting box. He was all in a huddle, right in the corner. 'Come on,' I whispered, 'it's time for a flight.' He didn't budge. His glassy brown eyes stared rigidly at me. I put food down. He still didn't move. After ten minutes, I ran to the phone.

'Mr Duckins,' I panted, 'Gregory Peck's not well!'

'Not well?' Alf repeated. 'Why, what's up?'

'He's sitting in the nest box and he won't come out!'

Alf paused to think. 'Have you *brought* him out?'

'No,' I said. 'If I put my hand near him he flaps a wing and goes WOO! really gruffly. It's just like he's on guard or something.'

'Oh, flipping heck . . .' Alf muttered quietly.

'Oh no,' I wailed, hearing that. 'He's not going to die, is he, Mr Duckins?'

'No,' Alf drawled, 'he's not going to die. Go back to the box and drag him out.'

'Then what do I do?'

'Put your tin hat on.'

'What?' I said.

Alf rattled with laughter. 'Just go back and drag him out.'

The phone clicked off. Confused, I hurtled back to the shed. Cherokee was pecking happily on the lawn. But Gregory Peck still hadn't moved. 'Come on,' I told him, reaching in, 'Mr Duckins said you've got to come out.'

Gregory Peck protested loudly. And when I managed to move him, I understood why. I gaped through the window at Cherokee Wonder, then into the nesting box again. Now I understood why they called them that. Mr Duckins was wrong: Gregory Peck still had some 'go' left in him. In the corner of the box was an untidy pile of twigs and feathers.

In the middle of the nest were two white eggs . . .

THE END

If you enjoyed this book, you might also enjoy reading about what happens next . . .

PAWNEE WARRIOR

by Chris d'Lacey

The paint was barely dry on my face, the gel still setting in my hair, the feathers rustling at the back of my neck. I had a red wolf's head on the front of my T-shirt. I was Pawnee.

How far would you go to protect what you love, even if it is a baby pigeon? For Darryl, facing up to his deadliest enemy, it might just mean his life. But sometimes you have to stand up and be counted. Sometimes, you have to be a warrior . . .

0 552 547883

ABOUT THE AUTHOR

Chris d'Lacey was born in Malta in 1954. This makes him a sort of Malteser, which probably explains why he eats so much chocolate. He began writing children's books in 1993. Chris's favourite subjects are animals, aliens, music and football – but not necessarily in that order. He also keeps pigeons.

One day, a long time ago, he found a pigeon with a broken wing. He took it home for 'a few days' to look after it – and ended up keeping it for fourteen years. He called the pigeon Gregory Peck, after the name of a famous actor. It seemed quite funny at the time.

Gregory Peck, the pigeon, died on Christmas Day, 1997. In their fourteen years together, Gregory and his mate Gigi managed to bring several young pigeons into the world, one of whom was known as Cherokee. This is not Cherokee's story *exactly*, but the way Chris imagines it might have been if he'd found a pigeon when he was a boy . . .